Praise for
The Sky Road Trilogy

Reader's Favorite – 5 Star Review

"… Hurst breathes authenticity into an ancient world. Each character has been crafted to become a friend or family member. To read Y'keta is to become one of the People."

5 Star Review - In'Dtale Magazine

"… Y'Keta offers an intriguing story with a solid setting. A coming-of-age story that while different also feels familiar, yet in a good way."

Amazon Reviews

"… breathtakingly beautiful."

"… well-crafted, poetic, and deeply moving."

"…takes the reader through that last rush from childhood into young adulthood."

EXILE

By Sandra Hurst

Dedication

This book is for my Dad, with love always.

and for Mum, who isn't gone;

just walking the Sky Road ahead of us.

A Note on Pronunciation

For people who, like me, want to know 'how to say it properly', I have included a pronunciation guide at the end of this work.

© 2016 Sandra Hurst - Sky Road Publications
www.delusionsofliteracy.com
Facebook: @SandraHurst-Author
Twitter: _SandraHurst

SPRING

One

First moon of Spring

<<<Siann>>>

Boom, boom, stop. Boom, boom, stop. Beating drums echoed the hearts of the People. I was only sixteen that night, and not a child—no matter what my mother thought.

The first moon of spring had trod the Sky Lord's path the night before, and today the Kit'na had come. They made their way to Esquialt from their home villages, hoping that by the end of the last winter moon the Salixt, Eldest shaman, would find them worthy of Walking the Sky Road with the People.

Over the past few days, the young men and women from the village had left to follow the ancient paths. They would pledge themselves as Kit'na to other villages further down the Coast, or even inland. If they returned it would be as treasured friends, still loved and never forgotten, but no longer family.

Matra stepped out in front of the fire. Her dark hair sparkled as orange flames danced with the copper beads threaded through it. The Elder Stars shone above her. She stepped into the fire-lit circle. Her movements perfectly in time with the heartbeat rhythm of the drums. Step, step, stop. Step, step, stop. Tonight, she wasn't just my mother, she was the Salixt, the one who hears the Lightning. The Salixt looked deep into the midnight sky, gesturing toward the six bright stars dancing overhead. "We are here, my children, on the night of the Great Dance. Over our heads, the Waki'tani soar, above them the Sky Road leads to the Elder Stars where dwell the Sky Lords—Ever Watching." For just a second, a brilliant flash painted the clearing with a white ghost light.

"The Sky Lords are watching," the people chanted, an unintended echo.

In the space between drumbeats, Matra spoke again. "The Kit'na have come among us, as they have always come, seeking to walk our Road in this life, and, at the end of life, to join us on the Sky Road." She looked intently at the newcomers standing just outside the firelight. "Let us welcome them, my children. See if their steps can become one with our dance."

The children of the tribe stepped into the fire circle. A warm spring wind ruffled their costumes of green feathers as they proudly flapped their hand-stitched wings. Surrounding the newcomers, they pulled them into a merry dance around the campfire, their piping voices a bright counterpoint to the deep heartbeat of the drums.

"We are the little ones, only begun;
Hatchlings know nothing of what is ahead
Send us protectors, who while we are young
Will stand between us and the darkness we dread.
As we take our first steps on the Sky Road."

Taking green feathers from their costumes, they presented one to each of the Kit'na and, laughing, stepped out of the firelight. I remember how the drums sped up then. My heart kept time as the Warriors of the Red Lodge emerged from the darkness beyond the campfire. War and blood were in their eyes and they carried the spears and arrows of their calling. Their voices rang like starlight on cold metal.

"We are the guardians, strength of the sky;
We walk the dark places, fight fear in the night.
Will you walk beside us to serve and to die;
To hold safe the People, keep honour alight
As we take up our spears on the Sky Road."

The Warriors handed a red feather—the tip sharpened, bloodied in battle—to each newcomer, bowed, and melted into the darkness around the campfire.

Grey as smoke, the old ones came. The Elders, the seekers, and more. Their slow steps and cracked voices made hardly an echo in the night, but each word rang clear.

"We are the Elders, our path nearly done,
Our wisdom and knowledge, we bring
Will you learn our dances, remember our song,
Let our winter bring grace to your spring?
As we walk evermore on the Sky Road."

With the presentation of the grey feathers, the drums fell silent and the Kit'na found themselves alone in the ring of firelight.

"Choose," the Salixt said, her voice echoing from the darkness, "and be known by the choosing."

A rangy woman with flaxen blond hair and cold green eyes spoke first. She stood among the Kit'na with violence, like a thunderstorm, filling the air around her. "My name is Ren, I am a warrior," she said in a voice as sharp and unyielding as winter wind, "neither a twig nor a creaking branch. I choose the way of the spear." With a bow, she set aside the green and grey feathers, strode out of the campfire, and joined the Warriors in the shadows.

She knelt before the red-haired warrior leader, saying, "I come to serve."

"Enter in," he replied. "Among the People, you will be called Ren Ut'yaat—Ren of the Forest Eyes."

The next Kit'na stepped forward, a slight young man in grey leggings and a tattered black vest which almost—but didn't quite—hid the fine scars and yellowing bruises on his arms and chest. His hair was black as a starless night, with a touch of blue-green when the firelight hit it exactly right.

For a long moment, he didn't speak, just stared into the campfire, seeing something in the smoke that no one else could. He laid the grey feather and the red one at the edge of the crackling blaze and watched them burn in smoky silence. Bowing towards the smouldering feathers, he turned to Iamaat, the eldest of the Mothers. "I am Varas," he said, in a voice a bit deeper than I expected for someone who looked so young. "I was born far from here. My village was inland, where the mountains are higher and the trees not so many. My village is gone now. That Road has ended. The children's songs I learned will be unsung unless other children learn them." His dark eyes flicked from child to child around the campfire, watching them watch him—some interested, some a bit frightened, some just sleepy, leaning on the adults to try to stay awake. "Will you accept me? I am strange to you. I know. Even so, there are things I can teach, and much I can learn."

Iamaat's hand rested in blessing on his head. "Be welcome among us, Son of the Forest, Son of our Village, be welcome home." At her blessing, the bravest of the children surged forward to surround Varas, their piping voices shrill and warm with welcome. Grabbing his hands, they led him to the edge of the firelight and pulled him down to sit on the trampled grass with them.

The last wanderer who stepped into the fire-lit circle surprised me. He seemed old for one of the Kit'na. The strong, muscled arms and broad shoulders were those of a man in full strength, like my father had been, not a youth starting out on his Road. His spiky black hair held touches of silver, and his eyes were the calm grey of a winter sky. "I am not Kit'na," he stated. "I left this village many cycles ago to become one with the people of Atiskaat, on the seacoast far south of here." He sighed heavily, closing his sombre eyes for a moment. "I thought my parents might still be alive. I hoped to see them at this ceremony."

The Salixt stepped into the fire-lit circle, drawing all eyes and creating a moment where nothing spoke except the campfire. "Your father stepped upon the Road some years ago, Laban, once of this village. Your mother is still among us though too frail for campfires on many nights. We will take you to her shortly."

"I thank you, Salixt," Laban said thickly. "An unexpected blessing. I am here, though, not only as a wanderer returned, but to seek your permission to learn from the Elders of this village. My village recently lost its Elder Shaman in an accident. There is no one with the knowledge to train another, and the village must have someone to speak for the Lightning and perform the rituals at cycle's end. I am the eldest of those who wear the grey feather. Will you accept me? I seek to learn the mysteries and then return to Atiskaat as their Elder Shaman."

The Salixt stretched her hands towards Laban. The backs of her hands were crepey and covered with lines. *But her hands had always been supple and smooth*, I thought. *When did she become an Elder? She's just Maskim, just my mother.*

Matra grabbed Laban's hands firmly, looked up to the twinkling Elder Stars, and with a joyful shout, she welcomed the Wanderer home. "Laban walks among us once more, let us welcome him as an Elder. Let those who walk with me in the cloak of grey feathers prepare him for the Road he will walk as Shaman."

As the cheering ended and the feast for the new tribesmen began, I heard my mother sigh under her breath. "Three Kit'na, only three.

Have the Sky Lords forgotten our village? Have we displeased them?" The uncertainty in her voice broke my heart.

When Matra left the fire circle, it signaled the end of the feast. Most of the villagers trudged wearily into their lodges and rolled into their blankets. Everyone had stuffed themselves with food and gone soggy around the edges from the berry wine the cooks had been fermenting since last summer.

§

The Elders were chatting around the fire when a sturdy young man marched out of the darkness. He strode across the campfire circle to plant himself in front of my mother with his fists clenched defiantly on his hips. His eyes were gold and rimmed with a black deeper than the darkness beyond the campfire; they seemed to glow yellow in the firelight. "I come as Kit'na to this village," the intruder said.

I glared at the brash young man. D'vhan growled in warning and took a protective stance beside Matra. The newest warrior, Ren, immediately shadowed D'vhan's posture, covering the left side of the clearing as he guarded the right. The stranger retreated, raising his hands, palms outward, to the watching warriors.

"I mean no harm." The brash young man protested, "I came late to the ceremony; the woods are unfamiliar, and I got lost. I am Y'keta, of the cliff dwellings in the far north. Your dance is strange to me, and I may stumble in the learning, but I come to learn from your people and to walk your Road."

"Why come to our village, Y'keta?" Matra inquired. "It is a long trek from the Ice-lands to these seas."

"I have learned all I can in my village. We see few strangers, and our storytellers know few stories beyond our own. However, they tell the tales of Esquialt, and of the things the Sky Lords have done here." Y'keta looked at the Elder Stars in the Northern Sky. "My people also believe the Sky Lords dwell in those stars. When they join in our springtime dance, the Road to the Ancient World opens for just a few moments and allows the People to walk the Sky Road. I would sit with your people and learn their wisdom, fight their battles, hear their songs."

"What say you?" The Salixt asked of the leaders of the three Feather Lodges, "Can you accept a newcomer who is so strange to our ways? Can you teach him what he can learn and forgive the things he cannot?"

Y'keta hung his head, awaiting the judgment of the leaders. I thought he was trying to look brave, but with his long arms wrapped around his chest and his straggly blond hair matted down his back, he looked more like a hatchling begging for treats he knew he shouldn't have.

The campfire was starting to falter. The smoke twining around Y'keta's feet like it was seeking him out, moving against the whisper of wind.

D'vhan, the leader of the Red Lodge, was the first to break the ashy silence. "To learn is never a bad thing," he rasped. "If the young one has traveled this far to learn, I am willing to teach." He took a blood-tipped red feather and placed it in Y'keta's hand. "Come," he grated. "Come, and learn."

The eldest Mother stepped forward, the green feathers of her cloak swaying. "I am Iamaat," she said in a voice unused to the stern tone it now carried. I smiled as she piloted her bulky frame to the centre of the fire-lit circle, squeezing between two children who dodged out of her way. "I am tasked with protecting and rearing our children, keeping our stories and ways for the future. We do not know you, Y'keta of the North. You are not from one of our tribes, and you have come among us with no introduction. I have no guarantee of safety for our little ones."

With a brisk, unexpected snap of her wrist, she took a green feather from the depths of her heavily beaded cloak and broke it in two, dropping it just short of Y'keta's outstretched hand. "I will not accept you. You may have skills and abilities which work well for a Warrior, but the children need other things; protection, gentleness, honour. I do not know you."

Y'keta's arms clenched tightly around his chest and, for a moment I thought I saw tears in his strangely coloured eyes. No one else seemed to pay attention. Even so, when those eyes passed over me with a sweeping glance, I noticed. I saw hurt, humiliation, anger, but not tears.

The issue seemed to be settled for everyone except the ramrod of a youth staring at the fire, furious eyes blazing. The Elders turned away, authority falling from them as the campfire guttered. Once more, they became just the villagers who I had known all my life.

I'm not sure why, but the sight of him standing there, fists clenched, shaking with fury at being dismissed by the Elders, pushed me a few steps further towards the firelight. "Who was the first?" I said shakily from the darkness. The Elders could not have looked more surprised if the campfire had spoken or if the Elder Stars themselves had come down to reprove them.

"Siann!" My mother sounded mortified, and since she was an Elder—and the village Shaman—it didn't bode well for my happiness over the next few moments. "This is Elder Council. Children have no place speaking here; even being here!"

A child! Always a child! "I'm past my sixteenth summer," I mumbled under my breath. "In a cycle or two, I'll be old enough to choose a mate or to walk away from Esquialt to become Kit'na elsewhere. Old enough to earn my place."

"Please, Mother. I mean no disrespect. You know I am studying our history and traditions and this," I gestured broadly from Iamaat, whose face seemed carved of granite, to Y'keta staring silently at the fire, eyes blazing with hurt and humiliation, "has raised a question."

Iamaat peered at me through the smoke. I could almost hear her dismissing me and any comment I might have, to the level of one of her green feathers, the babies of the tribe. She raised an eyebrow at Matra. "You already teach Siann the ways of the Grey Feather?"

Matra's gentle smile didn't hide the sadness in her deep brown eyes. "My mother left us last Cycle and Siann is the last in our line. She will become Salixt when I Walk the Sky Road. It is none too soon for her to start learning our history."

Iamaat spluttered, "It is not appropriate for a child to speak at council."

"You always taught us," D'vhan interjected slyly, speaking to Matra, but throwing a merry wink at where I stood in the shadows, "that to ask questions, whether appropriate or not, was the first part of learning."

Matra laughed merrily. "It seems I am caught by my words. What was your question, my daughter?"

Seeing the conversation had turned in my favor, I ventured further into the dying firelight, smoothing down my once-tidy tunic, now a mess of berry stains and ash. "I wanted to know who the first Kit'na was. Someone had to start the tradition. To walk from their village into a village that, like us, had no reason to trust a stranger." I tried hard not to stare too directly at Iamaat, instead giving a pointed, disapproving look to the ground in front of her pudgy feet.

"Very well," Matra said, "on behalf of the Grey, we welcome you to our village, Y'keta. To learn, to teach, and to share in all the roads we walk." She gave a nod to Iamaat, who was standing still and watchful, between Y'keta and the children's lodge. "I respect our Mother's decision. Until you have earned her trust, the Lodges of the Green Feather are forbidden to you. You will learn from the Red and the Grey and prove your heart is one with the People. However, we will be watching you."

Y'keta nodded at the shaman and then almost, but not quite, bowed to where I stood just within the guttering light. "My thanks, hatchling."

The arrogant, insolent, jumped-up Kit'na, I raged throwing a sharp-edged glare at the ungrateful slug. He looks no more than two cycles older than me, and he calls me a hatchling! After I defended him to the Elders, risking a severe reprimand from my mother on his behalf! Lightning burn him!

The Shaman gestured at Y'keta. "Go with D'vhan. He will find a place among the red feathers where you can sleep. Tomorrow we will see where your heart lies and what lessons you can learn, and what lessons we can."

It must have been an illusion. For a moment, I thought the smoke from the main campfire seemed to trail after Y'keta, twining around his ankles as the ungrateful slug followed D'vhan towards the Lodge of the Red Feathers.

Two

First Hunt

Y'keta watched as Siann stormed out of the firelight muttering under her breath., then followed D'vhan across the darkened clearing, trying not to stare at all the strangeness. Blinking owlishly, he ducked into the bright, warm interior of one of the lodges set around the central campfire.

As they entered the lodge, D'vhan dropped his bow along with the stern expression Y'keta had seen during the ceremony. He seemed to bubble with an underlying laughter; deep and echoing. *D'vhan,* Y'keta thought, *was the least warrior-like person he'd ever seen.*

"So what do I learn," Y'keta asked, trying to sound humble.

"The first lesson is sleep," D'vhan said, pushing him towards an empty pallet in the dim-lit area around the edge of the lodge. "I've seen more than one warrior on the wrong end of a spear because he was too tired to think when trouble started."

Smoke from the peat fire at the centre of the lodge combined with the smells of the campfire, tanned hides, and the four or five other warriors who slept there, to make Y'keta's stomach roil. Swallowing hard, he settled onto the sleeping furs D'vhan had given him and tried to understand what had happened during the ceremony.

I'm a Walker now, he thought to himself, gingerly removing his boots. *My feet tell me so. They ache and complain like an old man stuck outside in the rain.* He was unused to the punishment of a trail or the hours standing at the campfire while someone else–*Stars curse you, Father*–decided his fate.

D'vhan sauntered up and squatted beside Y'keta's pallet. "Rub this cream into your feet, it will help," he said, handing Y'keta a gourd full of some soapy-smelling mixture. "You are mincing around like the floor is covered with sharp rocks. We will be hunting in the morning and you'll need to keep up."

"Why are you helping me?" Y'keta demanded. "Iamaat distrusts me, even the Salixt doesn't know if I belong in this Village. Yet you go out of the way to welcome me and make me feel like I belong. It doesn't make sense."

D'vhan's teeth gleamed in the dark of the lodge. "Oh it certainly does make sense Kit'na." His smile was mischievous. "You just don't understand how yet." He stood up, stretching and bending his lanky frame. "Now, enough talk—see to your feet and then sleep!"

§

Y'keta was still half asleep when he pulled his soft-soled boots onto his aching feet. D'vhan, Ren, and one of the other Reds struggled out of the lodge and into the chilly spring air. Shivering, Y'keta followed.

"Grab your weapons and move out," D'vhan said, leading the small hunting party deeper into the inland forests. About an hour later, he called a halt, watching with subdued

amusement as Y'keta flopped down on a stump massaging his feet. "Are your feet still sore, Hatchling?" He laughed. "We'll get you toughened up soon enough." Bending down, he grabbed Y'keta's foot and examined the boots he was wearing. "Nice for the campsite," he said, "but these are not worth much on the trail. Ask me when we get back, and I'll show you how to reinforce them so your feet won't hurt so much."

D'vhan glanced around the small group and tugged thoughtfully at his spiky hair. "Pey't, Ren,"—he pointed to a trail veering off to the north—"try up there. Stay together and be back here before sundown. Y'keta and I will head south."

Pey't pushed himself to his feet with a grunt and nodded at Ren, who hadn't needed to sit down. "Come on, Kit'na, I want to catch our share and be back here in time for a nap before we walk home." D'vhan smiled as Pey't shooed Ren up the trail with grace and energy belying his size.

"Stop talking and get going Pey't." He chuckled. "I swear half of what we catch ends up in your bowl anyway!"

Watching them walk off down the trail, Y'keta felt his stomach clench and his heart crash through his chest. He had been counting on the commotion from a larger group to cover his lack of hunting skills. If it were just him and D'vhan, there would be nowhere to hide.

"Okay, Hatchling." D'vhan picked up his bow and gestured at the scrub brush. "Let's get moving. You need thick leather for the soles of your boots." D'vhan slipped noiselessly out of the clearing, leaving Y'keta to force a path through the sharp-smelling silversage and the tangles of wild roses.

The brambles tore and scratched at every exposed piece of Y'keta's skin, leaving him cursing and sore. *Why,* he thought, *had they seemed to move harmlessly out of the way of the elder warrior?*

After what felt like a lot of walking, but was only a few hours later, D'vhan dropped onto a moss-covered rock on the banks of a stream. They hadn't seen or heard anything; no birds, no deer, no small animals darting for cover in the brush. It was as if the forest were empty.

"Why aren't we hunting, D'vhan?" Y'keta asked, swatting at the swarms of insects hovering around the burbling stream. "The morning is passing quickly, and we haven't seen any game at all."

"Because," D'vhan's deep voice rattled like the rocks that were occasionally tossed around in the lively current, "the state of your boots and the way you fumble noisily around on the trail tells me you don't know how."

The constant knot of worry in Y'keta's stomach tied itself even tighter, and he felt the beginning of a thunderstorm of a headache.

"Now tell me the truth, Hatchling." D'vhan's dark eyes were not laughing anymore. "Why did you come to Esquialt? Why are you here?"

Y'keta's face flushed as he tried to find some way not to lie to the warrior leader. "I told the truth last night," he said. His odd-coloured eyes met D'vhan's with a predatory intensity. "All I ever wanted was to explore. To learn things beyond what my village knows. I took too many chances, and I was thrown out." He forced out the words with a gulp, "I can't talk about it. Please—not yet."

D'vhan studied Y'keta for a long, tense moment, nodded to himself and then jumped to his feet stretching luxuriously. His voice was low and gravelly, but not harsh. "A day will come when I need to know it all. On that day, I will insist. But you have told the truth for now. It is enough." One grizzled hand clapped Y'keta on the shoulder and gave him an ungentle shove toward the forest. "Let's get back to the village, Y'keta. Campfire will be started by the time we get back and I'm hungry. Some noisy hatchling scared away my first meal!" A few inches of shoe leather and a few hours of walking brought them back to the camp just as the morning duties ended, and the lodges divided up for training. "You will be joining the Greys after our meal," D'vhan informed him. "A bit of village history will be a good beginning for you."

As they crossed the campsite to enter the Grey Lodge, Y'keta saw the slight form of Siann duck inside carrying her scrolls and quills. *Oh, Shells!* he thought, unconsciously rubbing the back of his neck. *Lectures with that annoying hatchling, just what I need to make this day perfect.*

§

The evening meal was over and the campfire had died down. Several of the elders were quietly playing their reed flutes in the darkness and the villagers listened or chattered relaxing at the end of the day.

Iamaat stepped out of the shadows and stood between the flutes and the fires, her lined face shining in the flickering light. Gesturing to the children she settled them in a swarm around her, and the whole tribe fell silent to hear the mother speak.

"Listen little ones," she said to the young children sitting around her feet, her voice so quiet that the evening breeze strained to hear her, "to the cry of the Mourning Dove so soft and low in the forest. She has a story to tell us."

A very long time ago, when the forests were wider than they are today. A young woman named Juyaay was in the forest gathering seeds and berries for her grandmother's winter store. So many times her mother and grandmother had warned her to stay away from the deep forest. The people of the plains were not at home there and Juyaay did not know the languages of the forest creatures. It was late, and of course, laughing bird was too close to the forest, but that is where the best berries grew and she felt so proud when her grandmother praised her for bringing back a full basket.

Just inside the nearby forest, Juyaay saw a flash of black feathers and heard a harsh voice cry out, "Here! Here!" She looked at the branch where she had seen the black feathers and saw nothing, but at the base of that tree grew the best, juiciest berries that Juyaay had ever seen.

"I'm not that far into the forest," she thought, her soft brown eyes flashing around nervously. "I can still see the clearing from here." Sure that she could find her way home, Juyaay took her basket and stepped into the forest. "Only as far as this tree," she reassured herself. "Grandmother will love these berries, and I'm not so very far off the trail. She picked one of the wine dark Saskatoon berries, it tasted as juicy as it looked, so she happily picked all the ripe berries from under the tree and turned back towards the clearing.

"Here! Here!" The voice came again and she saw a flash of shiny black feathers and a bright yellow eye beckoning her from deeper in the forest.

The berries she had just picked were so sweet, she thought, maybe the ones further in were even bigger and juicier. "Who," she cried out to the echoing forest. "Who are you that keeps helping me find the best berries to impress my Kokum?" Which is the word the Plains People use for their grandmothers. Over and over

Juyaay followed the voice, never noticing that the clearing, and her way back to the village were falling further and further behind. She didn't see the black tail of Raven as he flew away laughing.

You can still hear her in the forest if you are quiet. They no longer call her Juyaay though; now they call her the Mourning Dove. She hops from bush to bush, always looking for the best and brightest berries, and cries "who? who? who?" looking for the edge of the woodlands that now, she cannot leave."

"Now children," the portly woman said. "What do we learn from the Mourning Dove?" Nut brown faces looked up some rubbing their eyes, others slumped on the shoulders of the older children.

"Listen to the Elders?" A little girl with green beads at the end of her braids piped hesitantly.

"A good lesson always," Iamaat nodded gently at the little one, "but not the one I was aiming for tonight. Anyone else care to guess at this most important lesson? No?" Her green eyes narrowed as she cast a meaningful glance around the fire circle. "Juyaay followed the Raven even though she didn't know him, she allowed a stranger to guide her. This is always dangerous."

Y'keta found himself drawn into Iamaat's story and when she was finished the silence had echoed in his mind like the wind through the canyons. Now he looked at the elderly Mother now sitting beside Matra frowning at something that the Salixt said. He knew Iamaat didn't trust him. Remembered the scathing reception from her when he had appeared at the Kit'na ceremony, surely this not so subtle warning to the tribe to distrust anyone strange was aimed at him, or at Matra for accepting him into Red Lodge.

Still, what she had woven between the fires deserved recognition. He skirted the campfire until he was standing beside Matra, a respectful distance from the green elder. "Mother," he said, holding his open hands in front of him as he addressed Iamaat. "I know we have much between us, but what you wove tonight was magical and it would be less than honourable for me not to say so." He bowed towards Iamaat and stepped back into the darkness, not demanding a result. Iamaat's green eyes flared and humphing angrily, she turned her back on Y'keta and the Salixt, lumbering into the darkness towards the Green Lodge.

Three

Unwelcome Discoveries
<<< Siann >>>

My morning started the way most cool spring mornings did, with a warm, full stomach, and the lingering taste of roasted grains and sweet dried berries. The camp came to life slowly as I watched, its regular rhythm just a little more sluggish than most mornings. My head was a bit fuzzy and it took me a few minutes to figure out why. On a thundery day, the ringing I felt in my ears would warn of a headache and send me running to Mother for one of her herbal mixtures. But last night's feast for the new arrivals had finished late, and mine wasn't the only pained face around the cooking fires this morning. The berry wine had been flowing freely, and many of the People had indulged. My festival tunic hung on the pole near my blankets, a tell-tale berry stain on the soft leather evidence of the cup of wine Uncle Pey't gave me to try at the feast. The unwelcome results had me squinting angrily at the pale sun.

I'd spent most of the morning amusing Napaay. We'd been playing with a cornhusk doll I made years ago and watching the children gather in front of the Green Lodge. It was strange to see Varas sitting among the children, occasionally reaching over to ruffle someone's hair or yank on a nearby braid, just like one of the little ones waiting for Iamaat to come out and set their lessons for the day.

Iamaat stepped out of the lodge and smiled at the cluster of upturned faces. "So my little ones," she said. "What shall we do today? Work? Play? Sing? Or just see where the Winds will blow us?"

A completely expected chorus of "Play, Play, Play" rose up from the dozen or so excited faces.

"Play is it then little ones?" Iamaat smiled. "And if we play all day, who will gather the wood? And if there is no wood, how will we make our dinner?" The little faces darkened, and brows scrunched up with suspicion. Was this a lecture?

"Here is my plan," she said, drawing an imaginary line from where Varas sat, through the group of squirming children and ending at her feet. "Those sitting on Varas' side of the line will go with him, those on my side, with me.

We will meet back here when the sun is three fingers over the trees. Whichever group has the most firewood, and berries will win the game. The winners will spend the afternoon learning new songs and dances from Varas." The new Kit'na's smile grew soft, grateful for a chance to share his history with the children.

"The losers," Iamaat paused for effect, "will spend the afternoon cleaning and mending for the Red Feathers!" Several of the little faces scowled at this prospect; that was hard work for small fingers.

Varas jumped to his feet shepherding the four or five bouncing children who had been on his side of Iamaat's invisible line. "Okay Warriors", he said, "let's go and earn an afternoon of fun!"

Iamaat's watchful gaze followed him as he marched his charges into the brush around the campfire. By the high-pitched giggles and occasional squeal coming from the brush outside the camp, it sounded like Varas had started a game of 'Fire Hunter' with the little ones. They had to gather kindling for the fire and then try to find where he hid in the brush to put the sticks in his pack. I laughed as Iamaat nodded at her troops. "Let's go little ones. They are getting ahead of us!" This was more like the Iamaat I remembered, not the stern almost cold woman from Y'keta's ceremony.

Mother stepped out of the Grey Lodge and waved us over. It wasn't easy to hear what she was saying over the green feathers whose rampaging yips and howls echoed through the camp. She made shooing gestures to Napaay who tripped over my feet as he escaped to the forest to play with the other Greens. "Well, Siann," she said once the stampede had quieted. "I see you no longer run with your brother and the other children when they head into the forest to play." With a nod to Iamaat, Matra gestured towards the cool cedar-scented quiet of the Grey Lodge and led me inside. "I know that for the last cycle you have been trying to have me see you as more than just a green feather, that you want to be treated as an adult," she said.

I couldn't believe what I was hearing! My heart raced and I pressed my lips together trying to force my surprise to not show. Since father had died three cycles ago, mother hadn't so much as hinted she saw any growth in me, no matter how desperately sensible I tried to be. Was she saying it was time for me to take on more responsibilities? To move towards adulthood? "What do you mean?" I asked, holding my breath in anticipation. "What kind of responsibility do you want me to have?" In my mind, I saw myself standing proudly in front of the campfire, speaking for the Grey Feathers, holding a new baby and announcing his name to the village, maybe even learning to do the Windspeaker rituals at year's end.

Matra chortled. "You are puffed up like a quail, all fluff and feathers, but with little meat to support its posturing. You are still the youngest of the Grey, my child, and far away from many of the things you will one day learn. Nevertheless, I think you have earned a chance to fly into a new challenge." Matra reached behind the sacred screen of the lodge and brought out a bundle of old cracked hide. Every possible space on the tattered surface was covered in ancient crabbed script. This was the parchment of the Waki'tani, our oldest legend. Our history taught us that the Sky Lords Walked in our village many lives ago. The scroll carried every word they spoke; no sign or action was forgotten. It had all been written down carefully, meticulously, so that future Shaman would recognize the Sky Lords when they next came. My hands trembled as I reached out to touch the brittle scroll with a reverent fingertip. "Not too much handling," Matra warned. "The parchment is extremely fragile, and the oil on your fingers will damage it."

I jerked my hand back and would have sat on the offending fingers, if I wasn't too old for such a babyish reaction.

"Your task, my daughter, is to transcribe this scroll onto fresh hide. Protect it from the dangers of age and damage from the weather."

Shards, I thought, well this wasn't what I wanted at all!

Mother placed a gentle hand on my arm. "This may not seem exciting to you, but this is the first task given any who train to become Salixt. I transcribed this scroll in my day, and now the task is yours. Do this well and you will be called on to read the Waki'tani scroll at the Winter Meeting of the villages."

I could feel my heart racing. "In front of all the villages!" I gasped. "Maskim, I don't think I can do it, what if I make a mistake?"

"If you transcribe thoughtfully and carefully," Mother said, smiling—I hadn't called her Maskim since I was a young child. "You will not only write the words on the hide but onto your heart and mind. Think of them, take them inside you and see if the power lives in these words. Finding the Lightning within is the first step on the path of the Salixt."

I must have gone pale as a winter hare because Maskim laughed and said, "Go and get some air before the rest of the Lodge arrives and it's time for last meal."

The afternoon sunlight must have blinded me because I didn't see anything as I pushed aside the thick hide flap and walked out of the lodge. Without thinking, I picked up my bag and headed to the north ridge to see if the berries there were ready for picking. Uncle Pey't liked them on his frybread in the mornings.

The forest was silent, quieter than anything I had ever noticed, or maybe the whole world had stopped to hear what Matra had said. *Was I to be Salixt?* It had gone unspoken since I was a child, but it still shocked me that she said the words. Could I be the one who heard the Lightning one day? Looking at the cloudy sky overhead, I tried to imagine the sound of Lightning. *What would it be like to hear it speak? To know the words in the Thunder were just for me, for my people.* I felt so small, so unsure. All my life I had read the scrolls and heard the stories, but I wasn't sure I believed them. How could I stand before the People and speak for the Lightning when I didn't know for sure whether anyone dwelt in the storms? *"Who are you that lives in the storms and Lightning of our mountains?"* I prayed just in case, not because I believed what the scrolls said, half daring someone to answer. No one answered, of course. No one ever did. No one answered when my father died. No one answered when the hunt failed and the People went hungry. Why should anyone answer now?

§

There was a light fog on the north ridge that seemed to get thicker as I walked further from the village. The new Kit'na would be at the campfire tonight. I just hoped they would keep mother busy enough not to notice my absence. Uncle Pey't was going to read the scroll of the Utlaak to the village, reminding themselves of the great danger of long ago. He would scowl at the ring of young faces around the campfire. They would stare back at him, half scared, half fascinated, as he told the tales of the enemy from Below.

It was here, he would remind them, that the last great battle in the war against the Under-dwellers, had ended. It was here when Esquialt was falling, its last warrior dead, that Surta, the Lord of the Waki'tani, the Sky People who flew between the earth and the Sky Lord's Road, had appeared to drive the Utlaak back into their barrows. The Waki'tani knew this Village's Road, Uncle Pey't would growl. There were even rumours that at times they walked here cloaked as warriors.

I was so tired of that story. I had heard it every spring camp since I was old enough to sit at the campfire. They came. We beat them. They came again. We beat them again. Why did it have to be anything more?

The legends weren't necessary, I thought. *Why is it important to keep retelling the same dusty stories just to feed the imaginations of the hatchlings and comfort the egos of rambling old men?*

§

The fog twined around the boles of the trees as I crawled in and out picking berries. It crept downhill and stretched its ephemeral talons towards the village. The afternoon had faded and the quick dusk of a spring night was falling. As the warmth of the day subsided, I pulled my shawl tighter around my shoulders. In the bush, I could hear crickets rubbing their legs together, their chirps slowing with the fog and wind. The ridge was steeper now, the black boles of the Aspens twisted and gnarled in the deepening twilight. I rubbed my arms as a chill breeze blew through the trees and looked back down the valley to the camp below. I don't remember coming so high or walking so far.

The fog carried the mouldy smell of the forest floor mixed with the nose-pinching bite of sweetgrass in bloom. Grabbing onto a thick aspen trunk, I pulled myself across the loose gravel scree on the hillside, following the strange fog up the ridge. Pebbles skittered down as I scrambled higher up on the sandstone ridge. They sounded much louder in the falling dark. I froze, hugging the damp, mottled bark of a twisted aspen until the sound faded and the faint noises of the forest restarted.

Hesitantly, I looked up the ridge. Though I squinted at it until my eyes ached, something in the shadows at the top of the ridge didn't quite seem to fit with the oncoming night. Yes—right there, between that boulder and the ridge line. There was something that didn't move, or should move, or something. It was just the wrong shape for a shadow.

The fog should have been thinner up here. It wasn't. My throat felt tight as I swallowed nervously. My feet were heavy and less willing to move the higher I climbed. The fog climbed with me. I don't believe in legends, I reminded myself. That's why I'm here. I don't believe the Utlaak wait in the dark or the Sky People steal you if you leave camp at night.

I finally reached the crest of the ridge and lay down shivering in the early spring moss. The damp vegetation soaked through my thick hide robe and chilled whatever courage I had left. *What was I doing up here?*

The fog flowed steadily toward the boulder where the black something hovered unmoving against the horizon. It wrapped around the twisted tree trunks and over my shoulders like a clammy stream; not still and airy the way fog should be, but always moving towards its ocean.

A scratching noise disturbed the forest silence. The shadow seemed to detach itself from the rock and extend itself to twice the height of one of the People. Great yellow eyes opened half-way up its body, swiveling backwards and forwards across the ridge. Sweat dripped down my face making my eyes sting as the creature carefully scanned my side of the ridge.

Breathing slowly just to keep myself from moving, I tried to see a form in the darkness. The rocks and soil under my fingernails felt hard and wet as my hands dug, attempting to find an anchor into the mulch; desperate for the reality of the cold frozen earth. Apparently unable to see anyone, the fierce eyes turned upwards for a moment, giving me time for a full, careful breath. A breath I abruptly lost as the amorphous shape seemed to split itself in two. Where the eyes had been was now the shape of a head with massive wings stretched out to each side.

The Waki'tani aren't real, I boggled, this isn't real! I've hit my head on a rock or a tree stump, and I'm unconscious; just lying here in the dirt.

Carefully pulling one hand to my side, I ran it over my wet braids checking for blood or bumps on my head, then I touched it to my chest feeling the reality of my own racing heart. I looked at the bird-shaped thing again.

The raven creature stood looking down at the village. Its wings spread wide in the darkness, blocking out the stars who were twinkling everywhere else in the frosty sky. Overhead, the Sky Road appeared, a million points of light showing the way to the Elder Stars.

The Waki'tani turned its head. I swallowed in fear as the great beak snapped at a passing thought. With a last look at the village and a noise somewhere between a human sigh and a raven's caw, it soared into the sky. For a few seconds, I could only watch as the creature disappeared into the distance, then, noticing the fog seemed to be evaporating as the creature departed, I scrambled from the ridge line into the cover of the lower bushes.

Clinging to the bole of a knotty pine tree, I tried to rebuild my world. It was a much larger, much scarier place than it seemed when I left camp a few hours ago. It was real, how can I tell them, it's all real!

Four

Rude Awakening

A rough hand rolled Y'keta out of his sleeping furs. Rubbing his bleary eyes, he tried to focus on D'vhan's unsmiling face. "What's wrong?" he grumped. "It's not my night to be on watch, and we only put out the campfire a few hours ago."

"Quiet," D'vhan hissed. "Wake Pey't, Sawiea, and Ren, and meet me outside. Bring your weapons."

"Shells," Y'keta cursed, suddenly not sleepy at all. Sawiea was the best tracker among the Red feathers. Village gossip said she could track a single raincloud through a thunderstorm. Pey't, although he looked more like an overstuffed pillow than a warrior, was lethal with both bow and knife. As he stepped into the damp night, Y'keta saw Matra and Iamaat, along with several of the Elders, both Grey and Red, shivering around the ashes of last night's fire. Scooping up some dry tinder, he knelt down, and with just a few quick movements with the flint restarted a small section of the campfire. Matra nodded her thanks as she clutched the sleeping furs around her cold shoulders and bent closer to the flames. Y'keta had earned a reputation in the two moons since he arrived; he could make a fire no matter how wet the tinder or how cold the day.

"Thank you, Y'keta," Matra said, turning back to face an unhappy looking Iamaat. The Green elder's puffy face was scrunched in an angry scowl.

"It's not our fight!" Iamaat said. Her sausage arms flailed angrily as she shrilled at Matra. "Why are we risking our warriors this way? There is no threat to our village."

"We are one People." Matra's voice was low and gritty. "What happened to you Iamaat? Why are you so frightened?"

Iamaat's ruddy face grew pale. "I am not afraid," she said. "I just don't see the threat to our village and I don't want any of my children risked unnecessarily."

"They are *all* our children." Matra reminded the Green Mother sadly. "The spear in your brother's heart *is* the spear in your own, we are one People. You taught that to me, to every child who ever came to the Green Lodge."

D'vhan strode up to the quarreling elders and Y'keta quickly ducked away from the smudgy firelight. "We're ready," D'vhan said, looking questioningly at Matra's thunder-filled expression. Iamaat gave a disgusted humph and clutching her blanket defensively, stomped back into the warmth of the Green Lodge.

"Warriors, fill your packs with drymeat and berries," D'vhan said. We will be travelling light and leaving within the hour."

As the warriors scattered through the camp to gather supplies, Y'keta saw D'vhan and Matra huddled together in earnest conversation. *The fire looks like it needs wood*, he thought and picked up a few pieces of dry seasoned wood, nonchalantly edging closer to the discussions.

"Come here, my children,"—Matra gestured solemnly to the collected elders—"and learn what has created such disturbance in the night." She was hardly an imposing sight standing there, hair in disarray and an old sleeping-fur clutched tightly around her bony shoulders. No one could dismiss Matra, though, not when the Lightning flashed in her eyes and her words held echoes of thunder. "A few moments ago, a messenger from Atiskaat ran into the village. She had been running full speed for the last two days and came with dire news. The Utlaak may have returned!" At Matra's words, the night sky seemed to darken, and the sounds of the sleeping camp became ominous rather than peaceful.

"A hunting party sent out from Atiskaat went missing. If it is our old enemy, there is a chance the scouts are dead and, if the Utlaak are behind it, their eyes have been taken." The Elders gasped in shock, and the faces of the Warriors gathering around the campfire went as grey as the ash floating in the damp air. The People had no greater fear. Without eyes, how would their spirits see to find the Sky Road. Even beyond life, they would be lost; forever seeking a way to rejoin their village.

D'vhan didn't speak. Rather, with a nod towards Matra, he led the Warriors towards the encircling darkness. The cold light of the stars on their faces showed or hid the tension as their natures demanded. At the edge of the clearing just outside the Grey Lodge, D'vhan stopped, struck the thick pole that marked the door, and waited until Laban came out. Laban was carrying not only a travel pack but also the ceremonial bundle of a shaman. His spiky hair was rumpled and dark. Streaks of ash marked his sternly controlled face; the markings of death and deep sorrow.

"Laban comes with us for the Grey," D'vhan informed the group of Warriors. "He is youngest of the Shaman and has the knowledge and strength to keep up with us on the trail." D'vhan's eyes pinned Ren. "You are responsible," he snapped.

Ren's head jerked, and her square jaw dropped open. "I have done nothing!" she protested, her sharp voice cutting through the night.

"Silence, Child," D'vhan's rumbling voice dropped so low it sounded like the rocks themselves were speaking. "Now is not the time for anger or self-justification. Once his training is complete, Laban will take his place as Salixt for Atiskaat. You will take no risks." D'vhan took a step towards Ren, looming over the slight young woman. "I have trusted you with the life of his village—do not fail."

Ren gulped, her wide green eyes silver in the starlight. D'vhan's large hands gripped her shoulders. "I know you have fears," he whispered for her ears only. "But you will not fail; it is not in your nature to fail."

He turned to address the warriors waiting in the darkness. "We travel by boat to Atiskaat. We will arrive there mid-morning and search for signs of the Utlaak barrow. If we find the bodies of the missing scouts, it is likely that they will have been mutilated. Laban and Ren will perform the ceremony to release the dead to join their village on the Sky Road."

§

The sun rose behind them, warming the cold backs and weary shoulders of the Warriors. They had travelled down the coast all night, the cedar dugout making steady progress as the paddlers took turns stretching out in the soggy bottom of the boat for a few hours of rest. D'vhan had left the wooden mast and sails in the village, just in case they found trouble in Atiskaat and had extra people for the voyage home.

They pulled the boat up onto the rocky beach and D'vhan stepped out, motioning Y'keta to join him. "Ren, you and Laban will head north. That is where the scouting party disappeared. Travel three fingers along the beach and wait for us." D'vhan's black eyes speared Ren with a glance. "Take no chances!"

Ren nodded, looked at the rising sun, and held her palm up against the horizon. "The sun is two fingers over the horizon now. No matter how far we have travelled, when it is at five fingers we will stop and wait for you."

"Watch the rocks and the bushes. If this is our old enemy, they strike from beneath the ground. Caves and gullies are as natural to them as the forest is to us," D'vhan warned. "We will speak to the Eldest of this village and then follow you."

"Sawiea and Pey't." D'vhan turned to the warriors still sitting in the dugout. Pey't wore the same changeless smile he always wore, content to wait for instructions. Sawiea sat stroking the dangling braids hanging from the tip of her longbow.

D'vhan remembered the night Sawiea had come to him asking to join the Red Feathers. Her mate dead, her only son gone years before to become Kit'na to a village inland. "I am not a Grey Feather or a Green," she had grumbled. "I cannot sit beside the fire singing songs to the children and waiting for the Road to call me." Taking her into the Red Lodge was somewhat untraditional—a widow, a mother, a warrior— but she had proven herself in battle many times. Her ability to track and her bow, with its decorations of human hair, had become legends.

"Take the dugout and travel south until you find where the river comes out of the forest," D'vhan instructed. Sawiea nodded, remembering a raging mountain river they had passed a few moments before reaching Atiskaat. "Beach there and travel inland. Follow the river and see if you can find any sign of the missing scouting party. No exploring," D'vhan commanded. "By nightfall, I want you both to meet us three fingers north of here. Pey't, keep Sawiea out of trouble."

Y'keta and D'vhan watched the two scouting parties move away from the village. Ren and Laban walking along the beach talking quietly. Faint sounds of laughter from Pey't and cursing from Sawiea as they paddled hard, forcing the cedar dugout against the current and south towards the river mouth.

§

D'vhan seemed unsure as they walked toward the waking village, not something Y'keta was accustomed to. D'vhan was stern, intimidating, and direct when he was acting as the leader of the Red Feathers. He had a much gentler, more joyful manner when he was at rest, although those outside the Lodge would not believe it. *Still,* Y'keta thought, *I have seen him angry, stern, happy. I've never seen him nervous.*

Standing beside the ashes of what must have been last night's campfire, D'vhan raised his voice in the ritual greeting. "Hail, Atiskaat. We come from the road." The flaps of the nearby lodges rustled. Y'keta smiled at the small curious faces peeking around the tent flaps only to laugh as they were shushed and hustled back inside.

"Hail, Stranger." An elderly woman, twig thin and frail, stepped out of the largest of the lodges. She moved with a stooped and careful shuffle which spoke of long frailty. "I am Siamaat, Mother of this village. What news do you bring from the Road?"

"I am D'vhan. I greet you, Siamaat, from Matra of the Esquialt." He glanced at Y'keta apologetically. "And I rejoice to see you after all these years. I was once Dovhan, a green feather under your care."

Siamaat's faded blue eyes squinted against the early morning sun. "Dovhan? Imrait's son?" She rubbed her hands over her face, the gnarled fingers succeeding in scrubbing ash and grit into her eyes, worsening their already irritated redness. "Matra sends you?" her voice was as cracked and dry as the dead campfire. "Did she send Laban? We need Laban! The Utlaak have our hunters, they will take their Eyes!"

Y'keta felt so helpless. The elder seemed incoherent, overrun with sorrow. She was lost in the tragedy of the Utlaak attack, and without a Salixt to anchor her, she couldn't move past the horror to lead her people.

"Laban is here, Mother," D'vhan reassured her. He placed his large hands over her bony claws, stilling the frantic gesturing. "He has gone with one of my warriors to find the bodies of the hunters, and together they will see them on the Road."

"But their eyes, Dovhan," Siamaat quavered. "If the Utlaak have taken their eyes, how will they find their way to the Sky Road?" Once more, Siamaat seemed to be working herself into a panic, her arms flapping wildly.

"Laban knows, Mother." D'vhan tried again to focus her attention on his face rather than the frantic whirlwind of thoughts obsessing her.

"Matra of the Esquialt has taught him the ritual; the hunters will find their way. Our people will Walk the Sky Road together." Picking up his pack, he gestured to Y'keta. "We go now to meet with Laban. We will find your lost children and see them safely on the Road."

§

Ren walked up the beach with Laban, her cold green eyes searching the woods for signs of the missing scouting party or damage left by intruders. Broken branches, dead animals, the sharp smell of trampled plants—all would tell if strangers crashed through without showing respect for the forest.

"Why are you here, Ren?" Laban wondered, "Why did D'vhan insist on you accompanying me and not one of the other warriors?"

Ren bristled. "Why? Am I not good enough to protect you?" Her long-fingered hands shoved angrily into her sun-bleached hair. "There is nothing any of the other Warriors can do which I cannot."

"I do not doubt you," Laban said, "it just seemed odd D'vhan was so insistent." Ren didn't answer. She turned from the rocky beach and entered the woods, leaving Laban to follow if he would. "What did you see," he asked. "Is there something near here?"

"The forest feels wrong. Mind your voice," she whispered. "We may be close now." Ren pulled a sharp dagger from her kaal-hide breeches, and her shoulders instantly straightened. Once she had a weapon in her hand, she appeared completely confident. *I'm no good at words*, she thought. *Laban wants to know things, and I can't explain.*

The forest was quiet, dappled light falling between the trees. The sharp smell of crushed vegetation and churned-up leaves and moss hung in the still air. A hint of an animal trail broke through the brush across their path. *Maybe a kaal,* she thought. It was something small, light-footed, certainly nothing significant enough to be a hunter, even a careful one. Finally coming across a recently used path, she motioned Laban to stop. "Something human-sized came this way. Not too long ago; one, maybe two days."

Laban slung his medicine pouch across his shoulders and drew his dagger. "Don't fear for me," he said. "I was a warrior long before I joined the Grey Lodge."

Ren snorted. "You are the heart of your village; Warrior or not. You will not be in danger while I can stand in front of you."

They followed the animal trail for a few turns until Ren held up her hand and sniffed the air. "Blood," she commented, the acrid copper smell making her nose wrinkle. They carefully pushed through an overgrown bush of silversage and into a large clearing; the site of the ambush. The bodies of the scouts from Atiskaat lay side by side on the grass, blinded eyes staring at them with mute reproach.

"I know them," Laban groaned. "Sun of Riad! I know them all."

He gestured at the bodies of a small woman and two men laid out like kindling across the clearing. "Mirad, sister of one of the Mothers in the village; Kaled, our warrior leader, and Jeddal." Laban swallowed hard. "Jeddal was a singer and the brother of Siamaat, Atiskaat's Eldest Mother."

The eyes of the hunters were gouged out. Dark empty sockets glared at the sky, reproving the Sky Lords for allowing such an atrocity. Laban pulled the ceremonial 'eyes' Matra had given him out of his traveling pack. "Take the stones," he told Ren, his voice faltering as he stepped out of his grief and into the authority of a shaman. "Place them in the eye sockets of the lost ones."

Ren took the stones from Laban, noticing for the first time how strong and powerful his hands were even with the tremors that shook him. The stones looked small in the palm of her hand; grey granite pebbles with bright blue and brown circles painted on them. *Eyes,* she thought, *he was giving back their eyes.* Placing the stones in their eye sockets as softly as she could, Ren stepped back, swatting away the inevitable flies, the bodyguards of death.

"Sky Lords, hear me," Laban intoned, walking to the corpse of the first villager and touching her face gently between the rock-hard eyes. "This is Mirad, daughter of our village, child of Atiskaat. Allow her the sight to find her way to the great Road. Welcome her to the Sky Road with her people."

He moved to Kaled. "This is a warrior, Great Ones," he said, touching Kaled's gnarled hands and drawing his dagger to place it on his chest. "Give him the strength to stand guard on the Road. Protect him as he has lived and died to protect the People."

His voice broke as he moved to the third body. Ren saw how hard he was trying, how much he needed to be a shaman at this moment, not just to be Laban. "Jeddal is here, Lords. Honour him! He is a minstrel, a singer of your songs and a walker in the dreams of your people. Take him with you on the Road. Let him dance with the stars." His voice remained strong as he released the souls of his friends to the Sky Road although the tears ran down his cheeks, mixed with the ashy markings of grief and despair. Reverently, Laban took the engraved flute hanging over Jeddal's shoulder. "His son should have this." He said heavily, "This is the least I can bring home." Finally turning away,

Laban fell to his knees. "Collect the stones, please. We may need them again," he said in a voice broken by sorrow. "We must find enough wood to make a pyre. We cannot leave their bodies to the animals and the wind."

"It is almost time to meet D'vhan on the beach," Ren said. Laban's eyes flashed.

"Then go," he snapped. "If my people are worth no more of your time." Turning his back angrily on Ren, he stalked straight-shouldered into the forest, and she could hear him chopping at the underbrush with his dagger. Still chanting prayers for the dead as he gathered wood for the pyre. Without a word, Ren put down her weapons and started dragging away the underbrush and piling wood and tinder, creating an open space in the clearing.

"I am with you," she said to the silent waves of pain rolling out of the forest. "You are not alone here with your people."

Five

The Eyes of the People

Siamaat watched with haunted eyes as D'vhan and Y'keta walked towards the beach. The cold wind plastered her robe against her emaciated body as she turned away to face the waiting villagers, hopeless.

D'vhan didn't dare to look back. Siamaat had been the Eldest Mother since he was a hatchling, had taught him to write and to read the scrolls. He had mourned her, thinking she had stepped on the Sky Road cycles ago. Now he was sorry she hadn't.

They headed north from the beach, looking for Ren and Laban. "How will you know where they left the beach?" Y'keta asked, looking confused. He swatted idly at the swarms of insects drawn out of the damp sand. "We could walk up and down this beach all morning."

"I know," D'vhan said his eyes appraising the young warrior, "because I have been studying woodcraft since I was a child. You are still learning." Y'keta's rubbed the back of his neck feeling the muscles in his shoulders bunch up. "We've spoken of this before, in Atiskaat. Now, Hatchling, tell me the truth. All of it." His voice dropped to a whisper, "Why are you here?"

Y'keta's face flushed. "I had to leave my village. I told you," he finally forced out with a gulp. "I disagreed with the chief, and the Elders banished me. They said if I would not learn from them, that I must walk to another village and try to learn from others." Hanging his head, Y'keta waited for D'vhan to renounce him, leaving him no place in Esquialt. If D'vhan would not accept him, Matra would surely cast him out.

"That must have been quite the argument, Y'keta. I can't imagine Matra casting someone out for just disagreeing." D'vhan waited patiently while Y'keta paced up and down the water's edge. His feet stomped the drying kelp and kicked angrily at the rocks. There was obviously more to this story.

Y'keta bent down and idly threw a few small stones, breaking the heavy silence. "My father is chief of our village," he finally said. "I was the second child. My sister, Netta, died in a skirmish with the Utlaak. It was my fault. I went wandering off, investigating an abandoned barrow; I wasn't there to protect her." Y'keta's voice was flat and emotionless, his arms wrapped tight around his chest. It looked like he would fly apart at any second and was holding on to try to prevent it. "Father thought me irresponsible and reckless even before Netta's death made me his heir. I was not allowed to hunt or to travel outside the village without guards." Y'keta's strange golden eyes blazed with anger as he recalled his last battle with Surta and his banishment to the Village. It had started when he heard his name spoken in someone else's conversation.

"Y'keta is Reckless!" Surta's voice came, muffled but easily recognizable, from inside the Council Roost. "Nothing I say affects him; he has no respect at all for my position!"

Y'keta shouldered his way through the entrance, his folded green wings brushing aside the vines that covered the lower entrance to the Roost. The interior of the council chamber was imposing—deliberately so. His golden eyes blinked rapidly, trying to adapt to the dim light from the large openings overhead. The light, filtered by vaulting arches, made the council chamber feel like a sacred space.

Neck-feathers puffing up aggressively, he stalked to the centre of the room. "If you're going to talk about me, Father," he snapped at the black-winged figure on the raised dais, "at least do it to my face!"

Surta stepped down from his perch, large black wings towering above him. "You are interrupting a council meeting; we will discuss your concerns later." His voice was clipped and stern as he peered down his hooked black beak at Y'keta.

"So you can talk about me to the council, but I am not allowed to hear what you have to say?" The bright green feathers on the top of Y'keta's head bristled in challenge as he stood, glaring up at his father.

Lightning rippled along Surta's wingtips, the hiss and crackle warning even the most foolhardy that he'd had enough. I've crossed the line, Y'keta thought. Shards, I've vaulted over it.

"Hatchling! You will leave now. We will inform you once the council has decided how to deal with your recklessness." Surta's sharp black beak bit the words in two.

Y'keta turned to leave, wings dragging on the floor behind him, talons making desultory scratching noises as he stalked away.

"I'm disappointed in you, Y'keta."

"Surprising," he sniped at his father, not bothering to look back.

§

Y'keta dropped slowly to the damp sand, shoulders weighed down by memories. "He wouldn't believe I don't want to be chief. So I challenged him in council, and here I am." The silence grew thick and stretched out, broken only by the flash of a dragonfly and the burbling of the water. "He won't accept who I am." Y'keta's voice was soft but still burnt with anger, "I can't accept who he wants me to be. No middle ground."

D'vhan watched hopelessness fall like a cloak across the shoulders of the sturdy young warrior. He let it settle for a few minutes and then grated quietly, "Did you ever think that your father could be right and wrong, at the same time?"

Y'keta raised his head, his beak-like nose and squarish brow wrinkled back like a dog trying to pick up a scent. "What do you mean, wrong and right?" He sulked. "Surta banished me!"

"He sent you here to learn, Hatchling. However, maybe the lessons you will find here are not the ones he intended for you." D'vhan put a gentle hand on the young man's head and watched as Y'keta tried to control an involuntary flinch. "I can teach you, but your first lesson must be honesty about who the Sky Lords made you to be." Brushing the sand and twigs from his leathers, D'vhan held out a wrinkled hand to the dejected Kit'na. "If you agree to be honest, with yourself and with me, I will count you as one of my warriors." Grasping Y'keta's wrist, D'vhan pulled with surprising strength, yanking the younger man to his feet and almost tumbling him into the surf. "You have a lot to learn about our ways. It will not be easy to put your pride away and learn as an adult what you should have learned as a child; but if you are willing, I will teach."

Y'keta grasped D'vhan's arm, forearm to forearm in the way he'd seen other warriors in the village greet each other. "I promise," he said, "I will try."

The grizzled hand clapped Y'keta on the shoulder and gave him an ungentle shove towards the forest. "Let's get back to work then, young hatchling. Laban and Ren are not far ahead of us."

"But didn't you say we would meet up on the beach at sundown?" Y'keta queried.

"Laban and Ren will head towards the beach for nightfall," D'vhan agreed, "but if they found anything in the forest, I want to see it before dark."

"You sneaky old crow," Y'keta spluttered. "You planned this just to find out about me!"

"Exactly," D'vhan cackled, the beads sparkling in his hair as he laughed. "Be wary of old crows. We are not as quick to fight as you young hawks, but infinitely more devious. Come on, Hatchling, you're wasting my time."

They walked north along the rocky beach for several hours. Only stopping when D'vhan spotted Sawiea and Pey't running back down the beach, the dugout canoe upturned on the rocky shore. Pey't didn't say anything, but pointed to a billow of oily smoke in the sky to the east.

"Follow," D'vhan grated, "but be careful." They moved quietly through the underbrush heading towards the plume of brownish smoke. As they crept closer to the oily smudge in the sky, Sawiea picked up a handful of dried leaves and tossed it in the air, looking at D'vhan.

"The wind is blowing from the south," she said.

"We'll approach from the northwest," D'vhan decided. "If this is the Utlaak, we don't want to give our position away until we are ready." As they slowly worked their way around to the north, D'vhan pointed out the flock of scavenger birds circling above the smoke. "Hania, the heralds of war. They are usually solitary hunters. If you ever see them in groups, there has been a battle, and the corpses are fresh."

The late afternoon sun is almost too bright, Y'keta thought. It seemed wrong when he knew they were approaching a place of death.

"Clearing ahead," D'vhan muttered, his red-handled knives already firmly in his hands. "Be ready." At D'vhan's signal, they burst through the underbrush and came to a crashing stop when they saw a funeral pyre.

Laban's shoulders straightened, but he didn't turn, just stared at the fire unnoticing. His eyes fixed on the remains of his people as they slowly returned to the wind and the forest. Ren looked up and nodded silently to D'vhan, then returned to the grim task of adding wood to the fire. It didn't take long for the intense heat and the stench from the pyre to drive the warriors out of the clearing and into the shade of the trees.

"Utlaak," Ren confirmed when it became evident Laban either would not or could not speak. "We found the scouting party at high sun. Their eyes were gouged out, left to the forest. Laban performed the ceremony to release their sight to the stars. We decided that being a little late to rendezvous was less important than this."

"As is right." D'vhan nodded solemnly. "It looks like the Utlaak headed this way." D'vhan pointed eastward to where the grass and trees showed signs of recent trampling.

"Even the forest rejects them," Pey't said, pointing out the blackened and broken plants marking the Utlaak's passing.

"This will take a few hours, D'vhan," Laban informed them bleakly. "Then we will have to bury what remains to keep it away from the beasts."

D'vhan nodded slowly. "We'll move on in the morning."

§

It did take a long time. Hour after miserable, silent hour, full of a stench Y'keta would never forget. Eventually, Laban allowed the pyre to die out, and they buried the scouts from Atiskaat beneath the clearing.

"The Sun of Riad will find them during the day, and the Sky Lords speak with them at night," Sawiea comforted. "It is well, Laban."

Night fell as Pey't was preparing a small meal. They ate, not speaking, and rolled into their furs.

"I've got first watch," D'vhan said. "No one sits watch for more than three fingers of the moon; then wake the next." Leaning back to prop himself against a tree, D'vhan wrapped his furs around his shoulders and set his red-handled knives across his knees. "You are after me, 'Keta, Get some sleep."

It took a few minutes, but the camp quieted and the soft sounds of a forest at night returned. Bushes rustled as a lean grey weasel pushed his way through the scrub to investigate the clearing. Casting left and right, it took a tentative nibble at Sawiea's leather boot. D'vhan's eyes twinkled merrily. Maybe it smelled the fish oils she rubbed into the soles to weatherproof them. The weasel must have hit toes because it skittered off in a panic as Sawiea rolled over, eyes alert and scanning the clearing.

"Go to sleep, Asawie," D'vhan whispered. "It's just your big feet attracting attention." Sawiea smiled sleepily at the old nickname, and muttering something about crows, pulled the furs back around her shoulders, and started snoring loudly.

The moon had risen a few fingers over the trees when D'vhan gently nudged Y'keta with his foot. "Your turn to watch. Wake me if anything seems out of place. Remember the Utlaak can't be too far away." Rolling himself up in his thick furs, he looked over his shoulder at the young warrior. "Sawiea after you, then Pey't. Let Ren and Laban sleep."

Y'keta rubbed his hands up and down his arms and wrapped himself in his fur and took up position against D'vhan's tree. He stared up at the silver-grey leaves dancing in the midnight wind. The Elder Stars shone overhead. He was at peace.

Three moons ago, he had been the chief's son; coddled, petted, rebellious, miserable. Now, here he was, sitting on a cold forest floor wrapped in stinky furs, about to stay up all night watching for enemies that had already taken three lives; he was happy. An owl hooting in the bushes startled him. Then a rabbit ran across the clearing, looked at the strange animals on the floor, and kept going. Finally, he decided it was time to wake Sawiea. Leaning down, he bumped against her shoulder whispering, "Sawiea, your..."

Before he could think, he found himself on the floor with Sawiea straddling his chest and a knife at his throat. "Hatchling...do not *ever* wake me that way!" Sawiea hissed from between clenched teeth. "Do you know how close to dead you were!"

Eyes huge in his face, Y'keta clambered out from under the spitting Warrior and backed away. Laughter filled the clearing as D'vhan, eyes wide awake and sparkling with mischief, chortled, "Use a stick and poke her; it's the only safe way."

"Are you awake enough to last ten more minutes, Y'keta?" Sawiea asked unapologetically.

"I am now," he responded from a safe distance.

"I'll be back, then." Sawiea said, "I'm stepping aside to scout around."

"Not too far out," D'vhan muttered. "Stay within sight of the clearing at all times."

"Roll over and go to sleep, old crow. Tonki is going with me." Picking up her longbow, Sawiea gently stroked the faded braids attached to its upper limb.

Y'keta frowned in the darkness. "You gave your bow a name?"

"There is a reason," Sawiea snapped as she stalked silently out of the clearing.

D'vhan was sitting up again, watching Sawiea disappear into the forest. "Don't push her, Hatchling. You are not the only one with a story to hide." For a few minutes, it was silent, broken only by the sound Sawiea made as she moved around in the scrub brush. "She's showing off," D'vhan chortled. "If she were actually scouting even the trees wouldn't know she was here." After a while, the night grew silent. D'vhan's face tightened as the moments passed. He started fidgeting with his knife handles, and muttering under his breath. The frown line between his black eyes grew deeper with each moment. Just as Y'keta saw him reach over to retie his boot lacings, there was a loud *whoot* from bush to the east of the clearing. "She's over there, and all's well," D'vhan said, sheathing his knives. He rolled his shoulders, stretched his neck from one side to the other, and commented, "We'll find out in a minute what she was up to."

The moon went behind a quickly moving cloud. When it emerged, the pale blue light showed Sawiea sitting on the ground beside them, as though she had never left. "So,

'Asawie," D'vhan asked nonchalantly. "What did you find walking in the woods?"

"Well," she explained, grinning at the pet name no one else dared use. "the nut crop is bad this year; the squirrels are complaining about working too hard. It's been dry, and the spider webs aren't as pretty as normal." Sawiea poked D'vhan playfully with the end of her bow. "Grey Weasel came by again but avoided the clearing; it smelled funny, something about your feet."

Picking up handfuls of dead grass from near his legs, D'vhan pelted Sawiea who laughed quietly and ducked out of the way. "Enough." He laughed breathily. "Report, Sawiea."

"Well," she said, somewhat abashedly, "I went around the clearing, as I said."

"Making enough noise to scare a Buffalo, I might add…" D'vhan interjected.

"Hmmph. Then I backtracked our ugly friends; the barrow is not far from here, maybe an hour's walk." Sawiea ducked her head rather than look at the frown on D'vhan's face.

"One day you will listen to me, old woman, and on that day…"

"And one day you will listen to me, old man," she replied, "and on that day you will learn something you may not ever forget."

With that, Sawiea kicked Pey't awake and rolled into her furs. Within two minutes, she was sleeping.

Y'keta shook his head. He would never have heard this kind of bantering and teasing at the Roost. You just did not speak like that to one of the Elders.

D'vhan smile to himself in the dark, noticing the Kit'na's confusion. "Don't worry about Sawiea. She is only playing. Sleep, Y'keta," D'vhan ordered. "Tomorrow may prove a difficult day."

Six

Siamaat's Revenge

The sun was barely peeping through the trees when the small war band approached to within sight of the Utlaak barrow, slowly working their way through the sparse cover. Y'keta tensed and loosened the muscles in his arms and legs, preparing for action. Carefully tightening the leather thong running from the shaft of his dagger to his wrist, he made sure the weapon would not get lost in the fight.

"You," D'vhan snapped at Y'keta. "Conceal yourself underneath this tree and observe. Whatever happens, remain hidden."

Y'keta bristled. He would not watch the others do battle while he stood back like a child. Pain flashed through him as the image of Netta's beautiful blue wings, shredded and bloody, stabbed his memory. He didn't do anything to prevent his sister's death. He couldn't sit by and do nothing now.

D'vhan fixed him with a glacial stare. "You are a warrior and under my command," he rumbled. "You will obey, or you will go back to the dugout to sit with the supplies." As D'vhan watched, Y'keta's shoulders slumped, and he seemed to grow smaller.

"I obey." The voice was petulant but subdued as Y'keta buried himself in the mulch and undergrowth at the base of the tree.

D'vhan laughed quietly, a sound like rocks rolling down a gravel cliff. "I did not ask you to like it. Obey and observe. Should all go wrong in this battle, it is your task to warn Esquialt. Matra will need what you learn here to help plan our defense."

Y'keta's eyes brightened at his words; they did not think him worthless and weak. D'vhan trusted him, had told him to take a scout position under these bushes and not to move, no matter what he saw. He was the eyes and the ears of the Salixt, D'vhan had warned him. He was to record, to remember and, above all, to stay alive.

Taking his place under the overhanging branches, he watched as the four warriors circled the open cave mouth and slowly moved inward. They seemed to be coordinating their approach with the small hand signs D'vhan was making. A raised hand and they inched forward.

A clenched fist and they became still, blending in with the trees surrounding them.

Wild cries broke the stillness. Three large Utlaak charged from the cave with maces and bladed spears in their hands. The spears were lethal; they ended in not one, but two sharp points. The knife-edged crystals embedded in the metal glistened in the morning sun. Not only would the spear pierce anyone it touched, but those crystal pieces would catch in the flesh, tearing savagely as the Utlaak pulled the spear back for another blow.

D'vhan rolled in front of Laban, pushing him to the forest floor as the largest of the Utlaak aimed at the shaman. "Down, Kit'na," he growled. "You may have been a warrior before you became a shaman in Atiskaat, but you are not a warrior now." D'vhan glanced at Ren, pointed at the flattened shaman, then back at the forest. Ren nodded, grabbed Laban by the back of his belt, and hauled him protesting out of the danger zone.

Y'keta watched Sawiea and Pey't dance with the scaly cave dwellers, leading them time and again from the shadow of the cave mouth into the bright sun, knowing their eyes could not adjust. Pey't's dagger sang as he dispatched the first enemy. A swift strike to the back of the leg, bringing the Utlaak down, then a jerk, a twist, and a fountain of greyish blood as he efficiently sliced the creature's throat.

Sawiea was a bit less gruesome with her target. A dagger into the thick hide of its back and the nightmarish creature lost the grip on its spear, letting it fly towards the tree above Y'keta. The spear whizzed close enough to clip the edge of Y'keta's dirty blond hair. But he stayed still.

D'vhan's knife made a squishy thud as it landed in the mulch near where Y'keta was watching. The warrior leader stepped lightly around a squat, slow-moving Utlaak. He looked like a young maiden dancing between the fires on a festival night; swaying and circling around a wizened Elder who had the spirit of the dance, but not the legs for it.

With each spin, there was a harsh, flat *thunk* as D'vhan's fist struck the Utlaak. It was a dance; nothing less could describe it. *Thunk*—a punch to the chest. The Utlaak gasped as D'vhan pulled the spear from its hands and threw it into the forest. Groan—another punch, this time to the kidneys as D'vhan spun past the floundering enemy to wheel behind him. *Thunk*—again a punch to the chest, leaving the Utlaak gasping for breath and looking around desperately for any way out of this bright nightmare and back into the safe, dark cave.

"D'vhan, down," Ren's nasal voice shouted from the fringe of the forest. Without hesitation, D'vhan dropped to the floor. An arrow flew past, inches above him, about where his throat would have been just seconds before. The Utlaak, which D'vhan had so carefully not killed, lay dead—fallen on its back, purblind eyes staring at the hated sun.

D'vhan whirled around angrily. "Do you think I wasted time dancing with this filth just so you could kill it for me? Who fired that arrow?" He looked from Ren, who was sitting on top of a wildly struggling Laban, to Sawiea, who for once didn't have her bow in her hand.

A dry cackle broke the awkward silence. Siamaat, the mother from Atiskaat, stepped out of the brush, a bow clutched in her gnarled fingers, her faded blue eyes more than a little mad. "I have avenged my children." She capered around the bodies of the Utlaak, shaking her bow and crooning to herself.

"Mother," D'vhan spoke slowly to the addled woman.

"Leave her to me," Laban said, brushing the dirt from the forest floor out of his eyes and casting a reproachful glare at Ren. "She was not always what you see now. Siamaat has been Mother to two generations of our children. I will speak with her and lead her home." Taking the babbling Elder by her hand, Laban started back towards the village.

"Ren, go with them," D'vhan ordered. "See the Elder reaches the village safely. Stay there until my return." He nodded towards the other warriors. "We will burn these corpses, scout the barrow, and return for you in two days."
Ren nodded followed Laban and Siamaat back into the forest.

D'vhan grabbed Y'keta, hauling him out from under the leaves and branches, then gave him a gentle shove towards where Pey't and Sawiea were digging a pit. "Help them deal with the corpses. I want no sign left for any other raiding party to find."

Dead bodies are inconvenient, Y'keta thought, *somehow it should be quicker than this.*

Sawiea gathered enough wood to start a decent fire in the pit, and they hauled the carcasses of the fallen Utlaak unceremoniously into the flames. By evening, the pyre was out, the ashes buried, and the clearing returned to normal. Only the blackened ground in front of the cave showed any sign a battle had happened there.

Collecting their weapons and those of the Utlaak, the warriors headed towards the boats. They would sleep on the beach tonight, scout around the barrow tomorrow, and on the next day pick up Ren and Laban for the long trip up the coast, towards home.

Matra had to be told of the barrow. It was the first time they had come so far down from the mountains in generations.

§

Walking back to Atiskaat is taking a long time, Ren thought. Laban led Siamaat by the hand, talking quietly to her while pointedly ignoring Ren.

"Laban," she queried, trying hard not to sound hurt or offended.

Laban looked at the rangy woman walking behind him and then turned back to Siamaat. "All will be well, Mother," he spoke soothingly to the distracted elder. "The lost ones have been returned to the People, and now all will be as it was."

Siamaat sobbed softly, her bony shoulders shaking. "What have I done, Laban? I am a Mother; I nurture life. I do not kill!"

"Mother Siamaat," Ren piped up, her sharp voice cutting through the silent forest, gaining a *humph* of disapproval from Laban. "What does Mother Grizzly say when her cubs are threatened? Or Mother Buffalo? You did what you should do!"

Siamaat looked around at the forest, her rheumy eyes finding things at once familiar and strange. "You are wise, young Ren," she said in a croaking voice, "and you are foolish, Laban, to blame Ren for obeying her leader in the middle of a crisis." Siamaat laughed, although a bit weakly, as the sun came out over the forest and the light danced on the leaves and filtered down to the path. "Where is Dovhan?" she said, seeming surprised the warrior leader was not following them.

"He and the Warriors will see to the dead and scout around the barrow, Elder," Ren answered. "They will return in two days to collect Laban and me." *That is*, she thought, *if Laban decides to come home.* She couldn't blame him if he stayed. This was his village, and it needed him desperately. Nevertheless, Laban was still several moons from finishing the training to become a shaman. He would not undergo the trials until the midwinter festival. Before he could return with the authority of a shaman, he had to Walk the Lightning.

Walking into Atiskaat was heartbreaking. People poured from the tents to surround Siamaat and Laban. Adult faces quiet and solemn, and children with their high-pitched voices running around to greet them. Ren stepped into the shadow of one of the lodges and watched from a carefully maintained distance. No one had ever run to her the way the children ran to Laban. Even as a child, her village treated her as a stranger. The Mothers raised her, she was one of their obligations, but she had always been alone, child of no one, her parents gone on the Road within days of her birth. Just as she was working her way into a deep black brood, Laban appeared before her.

"I'm sorry," he said, his grey eyes rueful. "Being pushed aside back at the barrow made me feel like a child. I hate that."

Ren gave him a half-smile and nodded. "Go to your people, Laban. We have to leave in a few days, and they need their time with you."

Later, in the quiet darkness of the woods, Ren would take out the memory. Laban lying face down on the forest floor, her sitting on his back, and she would smile, genuinely smile at the image. *He had looked like a child,* she thought. *It was perfect.*

She unrolled her sleeping furs and set them in a small clearing just outside the campsite. Drifting to sleep, she looked up at the stars and for one of the few times in her life, she prayed. *Sky Lords, if you do see me and know the Road I Walk, let me find a place where I belong. Where people are glad to see me, and where, like Laban, I can have roots in this world.*

Ren woke suddenly, startled by a sound in the darkness. Tightening her grip on her dagger and opening her eyes just a slit, she glanced around, careful not to move just in case she was being watched. She was. Laban was sitting at the edge of the clearing, watching her.

"What's wrong, Laban? Is something amiss in the village?" Her voice was husky with sleep and quiet enough not to wake the watching stars.

"Nothing wrong," Laban replied, "I just came to see where you were. But you looked so peaceful I couldn't disturb you."

"I needed some quiet," she said, "the past few days have been rough. I've never killed before. Not a man, enemy, whatever you call the Utlaak."

Laban scooted over to where she lay wrapped in her blankets, pulled a fur from his own pack, and laid down on the earth beside her. "Sleep," he urged quietly. "I think we both need it."

"But you have a lodge in the village." Ren questioned, "Why are you sleeping here?

"I stay with you. You are my responsibility, just as D'vhan made me yours."

Ren turned over with a sigh. Responsibility. She understood responsibility–though some part of her she would not admit to, maybe wanted something else.

A large furry arm flung across her shoulders and pulled her backwards until she was resting against Laban's hard chest. "You think too much," he growled in her ear. "Sleep!"

§

Morning came with the sound of crickets and the sweet melody of the frogs in the underbrush. Ren stretched, surprised to find she couldn't move. There was an arm locked about her, a warm snoring body behind her and, much appreciated on such a cold morning, an extra fur pulled carefully around her shoulders. No one could see her, so she felt safe to smile, close her eyes, and just for a moment pretend she belonged.

When she woke again, Ren found the furs tucked in tightly behind her and no sign of Laban anywhere. The sun was sneaking over the eastern edge of the glade, and her breath made white puffs whenever she exhaled. Rolling out of her fur cocoon and bending down to grab her travel pack, she stopped abruptly, mouth gaping open as she spotted a bundle of dried vair fruit; a rare delicacy this far north. The fruit rested on top of her pack with Laban's braided leather wristband wrapped around the stems, making the leathery dark-red globes look like flowers.

Ren pinched a berry from the vine and popped it into her already watering mouth. Eyes closed, she let the tart, winey flavour travel from her mouth, through her memories, and into the coldest part of her soul. She had tasted vair fruit once as a child. A trader had come to the village, and Gennet, the mother at that time, had traded a fur-edged blanket for enough berries so each of the children could have one taste. On that day, even Ren was included.

Wrapping the fruit carefully in her blanket, she packed up and walked into Atiskaat. Laban stood hunched over in the middle of the campground. He seemed to be using a long stick to draw in the dust in front of the Red Lodge. Ren was good at staying unnoticed. She learned early the art of becoming nobody, blending into any group of people invisibly. It had kept her alive in the rough and tumble after her parents left and Gennet, the Green Mother, had died. It made her a good hunter, and a great scout; at least, it usually did.

Laban lifted his head the instant she stepped around the corner of the Red Lodge. *I must have stepped on something,* she thought. He didn't look for her; he looked at her—directly at her. People didn't do that.

"Good morning, Ren." He smiled at her, running a long-fingered hand through his spiky black hair. "Would you come and look at this. Siamaat found something in the village scrolls that might be significant." Stepping aside, he made room for her to bend over the scratched-out symbols on the dusty floor.

"What am I looking at?" Ren asked, appearing puzzled.

Siamaat pointed at the ground with a bony finger and narrated, "This is the camp, south of us the river flows from here to here." Her finger moved from the mouth of the River west-northwest on the makeshift map. "About three days up the river is an extensive barrow. We've known about it for many years, and our warriors regularly go to make sure it is still unused. It has been the same since my grandmother's grandmother was the Mother to this village."

"It's empty?" Ren looked at the older woman in disbelief. "Utlaak seldom abandon a barrow; they keep at least a passageway open to make sure they can return."

"Laban can confirm it. For three generations, we have checked the barrow in spring and fall and seen nothing. Nevertheless, when we went this year, there was gravel in all the tunnels and new rock piled at the cave mouth. They are digging."

Ren and Laban looked at each other, their expressions mirrors of concern and anxiety. "Do you think the ones who attacked your scouts came from this barrow, Mother?" Ren asked, throwing a quick glance at Laban. It was actually Laban's place to ask, but the dead had been his friends, and she could spare him, at least, this much.

"We don't know of any other Utlaak den near here," Siamaat confirmed. "It had to be from the north barrow."

Laban rubbed at the deep ridge between his eyes. "Matra needs to know this now. I think we should start back towards the village," he suggested, "and let D'vhan find us on the way."

Ren didn't answer, just nodded and strapped her travel pack on her back. Nothing in her face betrayed how happy she was Laban had said *we*. He was coming back with her.

Grabbing a half-burnt stick from the campfire, Laban quickly used the charcoal end to sketch the barrow's location on a scrap of hide. "I'll tell Matra of this, and we'll send some warriors to help you until you can get enough Kit'na to replace the four who were lost." Laban rested a gentle hand on Siamaat's shoulder. "Farewell, Mother. I will see you at the midwinter festival." Gathering Ren up with his eyes, they moved out of the village at a trot. Laban waved farewell to the small faces peeping from the lodges and exchanged quick words with the adults. Laban was leaving home; not going home. Ren's heart sank.

It took no more than a few minutes to reach the stony beach and start moving north towards Esquialt. Ren shoved one hand into her travel pack and pulled out the wristband Laban had wrapped around the vair berries. Fixing her eyes on some invisible spot beyond the horizon, she offered it to him abruptly. "Thank you, for the berries." Her cheeks flushed as she tried to remember the manners that had been thumped into her as a child. "I appreciate the gift."

Laban's smile was gentle and older than his years. He slowly reached out a hand, as though approaching one of the half-wild dogs that sometimes followed the camps. "And I appreciate you. You made a great sadness easier to bear." Folding her fingers around the ornate wristband, he stepped back, allowing her room to escape.

Her eyes flashing frantically up and down the beach, in the air, anywhere but at Laban's smiling face. Ren let her breath out in a *whuff* of relief as she spotted a war canoe on the horizon. "Could that be D'vhan?" she asked in what she hoped was a neutral voice. Ren waved at the oncoming boat. She could see Pey't and Y'keta paddling, and spotted the familiar form of Sawiea waving her longbow in greeting.

Trying hard not to look at Laban, she waded into the surf and grabbed the prow of the boat. Dragging it up on the rocky shore, she reached down a hand to help D'vhan jump out.

"Why are you not waiting in the village?" D'vhan demanded tersely. "Is something wrong?"

"Possibly," Laban replied. "Siamaat told us of an active Utlaak barrow between here and Esquialt. I thought it important enough to start walking to meet you so we could get back to Matra quickly."

D'vhan looked thoughtfully at the young shaman and decided to trust Laban's instincts. "Get in," he ordered. "We'll start paddling back and push through the night to get home."

"I can take a turn at the paddle," Ren offered. *Something physical to do right now would be a blessing,* she thought. *I need some time under the Stars to figure out what happened on the beach.*

"As can I," Laban jumped in with a wry look.

Shards, Ren cursed to herself. *He knows I'm avoiding him, and he just won't let me wiggle away.*

Turning the boat from the shore, they started paddling upstream back towards Esquialt. "Keep the sun in your left eye and wake me at dark," D'vhan said. "I'll take over then."

Ren bent over her paddle and concentrated on the ripples it made as it dipped and swished in and out of the dark-green water. The soft sun-warmed smell of the cedar boat frame soothed her distracted thoughts and left her with a strange, tranquil feeling.

A splash of ice-cold water hit her on the side of her head, forcing Ren out of her daydream. She glared into Laban's laughing face. "Don't think so hard," he said. "Your face will stick like that."

Why the shell-headed, smart-mouthed... She had had enough! First, he warms her heart like no one has since she was a young child, leaves her a present worthy of a chief, embarrasses her by telling her to keep it, and now he wants to play! Well, she could play too! With the speed of a born hunter, she flicked her paddle, sending two handfuls of the icy water across the boat and into Laban's lap. Ren giggled madly as he let out a high-pitched squeal and looked at her reproachfully. "Brave Shaman," she taunted. "You love to play until someone retaliates!"

Soon both paddlers were soaked and laughing like children. They paddled on through the sunny afternoon, re-starting the war every now and then. Until Laban missed. "Shards!" he cursed.

D'vhan sat up and glared at them, thunderclouds circling his wet, drippy head. "What do you two crack-wits think you're doing?" Although he was usually the most reasonable of the Lodge Elders, he never did wake up gracefully. "I'm soaked! I should throw you out of the boat and let the Utlaak take you in!"

Ren turned away from the grouchy warrior leader, her shoulders slumping. Her paddle dug into the cold salt water as though to punish it for taking the time to play. Laban just looked at D'vhan's scrunched up face and wet hair and laughed merrily. "You'll dry out, D'vhan. There's no sense barking at us for enjoying ourselves. We did manage several hours of good paddling between dousings."

Finally taking a moment to check the position of the sky and the rocky coastline nearby, D'vhan let out an exasperated sigh. He couldn't be angry with them. They were over half-way home and had apparently kept a good pace despite their foolishness. "If you do anything like that to me again I'll send you to the Green Lodge for a month! My heart could give out from such a shock at my age!"

Sawiea's low melodic laugh defused the situation as she leaned forward to shove at D'vhan's shoulder with surprising strength. "Stop it, old crow. You aren't angry, you're just a grumpy old bird who hasn't eaten yet today!"

"Quiet woman," he growled. "You're giving away my secrets."

Tempest over, they journeyed home, laughing.

§

Dragging the boat onto the shore outside the village, the weary travellers trudged up the well-

beaten trail into camp. It was long past
moonrise. The crickets chirping in the forest
made an unintentional counterpoint to the *slap*
and *shush* of their boots on the pine-covered
trail. When they reached the centre of the camp,
they saw the campfire was dead, and no one was
stirring.

"Ah well, they weren't expecting us until
morning," D'vhan muttered. "Tomorrow will be
soon enough to worry Matra with a danger two
day's march away. Laban, make sure you don't
lose that scroll. We'll meet after first meal to
introduce Matra to her new neighbours."
D'vhan scratched his scraggly beard, and with a
yawn ducked to follow Y'keta, Pey't, and
Sawiea inside the Red Lodge.

As Ren turned to follow, Laban laid a
tentative hand on her arm murmuring, "Please,
don't go yet."

Ren's brow wrinkled in confusion. This
wasn't the assured shaman she knew—neither
did it sound like her playmate from the ride
home.

"I shouldn't ask," Laban murmured looking
around the dark campsite at anything that wasn't
Ren's face. "But would you...could you stay
with me? I'm not asking for anything, just
another human presence in the lodge. The faces
of those who died in Atiskaat are haunting me
tonight."

Ren looked at Laban. This powerful man who could speak with the Lightning, who stood for his people before the Sky Lords, needed her. Not Sawiea. Not D'vhan. He was hurting, and he needed her. Ren of no name, Ren with no family. Her.

It took more courage than she ever imagined she had to reach out and place her hand on Laban's cheek. "No one should be alone when the darkness is speaking. I will stay with you."

Beginnings are delicate things, Laban thought. Barely resting his arm on her shoulders, he turned her towards his empty lodge. Not holding her—it was far too fragile for that.

Stretching out his furs inside the lodge, he waited until Ren rolled herself into her fur cocoon. Her eyes were emeralds in the dim light of the small fire heating his lodge. Her guarded expression reminded him of the swift kaal they hunted on the plain, caught between running and freezing in panic. He made sure Ren saw he was fully dressed as he wrapped himself in his sleeping furs and spooned up close behind her. The fire was not bright enough to cast any light on their faces, so he lay there listening until her breathing finally softened, and she slept. Then, carefully, he wrapped an arm around Ren's waist and pulled her back against him and whispered "Thank you" into her long wheat-coloured hair.

Eyes closed, breathing controlled, Ren let her soul lean into his warmth. Somewhere a small spark flickered in her mind, and for once all the years spent cold and lonely could not stifle it.

Ren was gone when Laban awoke the next morning. Her furs were rolled into a neat bundle and tucked up beside him. *She tried to keep me warm.* He smiled to himself in the dim light, touched at her thoughtfulness.

§

Even for so early in the day, lazy grey plumes rose from smoky campfires, and the whole village showed signs of waking. The pale morning sun peeped around the great boles of the redwoods, warming the cedar-shakes roofs of the lodges. Blinking in the watery light, Laban stepped out of his lodge and tried to shake his mind into wakefulness. Matra, D'vhan, and Ren were standing on the other side of the clearing, drinking cups of the steaming herbal tea Matra was famous for. Dodging a few stray dogs, he worked his way to the group and stood behind Ren, who was drawing the map to the Utlaak barrow from memory.

"It looks like the barrow is about three days upriver from where we landed," she said to Matra. Ren's nose wrinkled as she struggled for accurate recall. "The Mother in Atiskaat said it has been abandoned for several generations." Unthinking, she flicked her hair over her shoulders and jumped when the pale braid connected with Laban's face. Flushing, she turned rapidly back to the map. "Just before the scouts were attacked, they reported fresh earth moving there."

"It was clear the Under-dwellers killed the scouts," Laban added. "Their eyes had been gouged out, and they were laid face up to the sun as though to rebuke the Sky Lords with their blindness." Ren felt a ripple of movement against her back as he swallowed thickly. "An animal or one of the People would not kill so."

Matra looked intently at the map drawn in the dust. "Do you have this on a parchment or hide?" Laban nodded and handed her the sketch they had made in Atiskaat.

Thanking Laban, she rolled the hide up and turned away. "I will take this to the Elders of the Grey Lodge. Maybe something in the scrolls from the last war will give us insight." As usual, Matra's black hair was braided with the red, grey, and green beads marking her as Eldest of the Village. Today, even their sparkle did not lighten the expression on her face. She was worried; it showed. "To our morning duties, children," she ordered, trying to re-establish some form of normalcy. "We will discuss this after the Grey Lodge has had time to compare it with the ancient scrolls."

SUMMER

Seven

Suspicions
<<<Siann>>>

The day unwound much like every day. I spent the morning looking after Napaay. We were supposed to be picking berries, but I spent most of my time pulling him out of briar bushes. It was a challenge trying to get at least a few of the berries I picked into my bag for the evening meal—most of them disappeared into his chubby blue-stained face. His name should have been Geeshoo. My brother, the piglet.

As the mid-day meal approached, I could finally leave Napaay with Iamaat and the other Green Feathers and start my work for the day. It surprised me to see my mother dawdling at the entrance of the Grey Lodge. I stepped past her out of the sunshine, eyes blinking, adjusting to the dim light. A moment later she followed me into the lodge, picked up an elaborate bouquet of flowers, and handed it to me.

"What is this for?" I looked suspiciously at the bouquet, holding it away from me as though it were infested with beetles. "Why are you giving me these? Can I see silversage in there? Who is sending me courtship flowers?"

"They are on behalf of Varas," Matra said. "Iamaat and I have spoken. We think it would be a suitable match and have told him that he is our choice to court you."

"Shells, Mother, why would you arrange such a thing without talking to me?" Storming into the section of the Grey Lodge set aside for our family, I threw the bouquet of sage flowers onto my bedroll with a smouldering glare.

"Siann! Don't you take that tone with me!" Matra's voice echoed from the main area of the lodge. "You know it's traditional. If there is one of the other Kit'na you would rather…"

"What I would rather? I would rather you not set up a mating for me like I was a fur you were trying to trade at the hunting grounds." I stomped around the small family area, but there was nothing here I could kick, and I desperately needed to kick something. Mother stood in front of the door, and even angry as I was, I wasn't going to push her out of the way. "Let me past, Mother," I said, glaring past her left shoulder. "I'm so angry I can't even look at you right now!"

"Be quiet, Siann, and listen for once," Matra said in her most annoyingly reasonable voice.

I wheeled around on my heel, kicked a stack of hides and scrolls, and cursed loudly when it hurt. "Mother, I'm not listening. I'm not quiet. And I. Am. Not. Going to end up mated to Varas!"

Matra rubbed her forehead and pinched her eyes closed. "Who said anything about mated? Both of you are a long way from ready. Iamaat and I just thought it might be good to explore possibilities."

"You and Iamaat thought? What about what I think, Mother? What about what Varas thinks?" I grabbed random pieces of clothing hanging from the pegs in the corner and started pulling them on over my loose inner tunic. "Here you sit blithely planning my life for me." My words were muffled as I pulled my warm outer tunic over my head. "Did you even think to ask what Varas wants?" I stomped my feet into my boots, ducked under Matra's restraining arm, and bolted. If I hadn't left, I'm sure I would have said or done something I couldn't take back. I grabbed my berry bag from the hook outside the door and charged straight through the village. Anyone who dared to stop or speak to me earned a glance crackling with lightning.

I stumbled as I passed the Green Lodge. Varas was outside talking to one of the younger children. He flashed me his usual sweet smile. I growled and moved faster. I pushed my way through the brambles and headed for the small lake just east of camp. I was careful not to head up the north ridge and risk a run-in with the raven creature I had seen there in the spring. *I can't do it,* I thought. *I don't care what Mother thinks. I am not ready to take a mate and settle in the village.* Especially now. I hadn't found the courage to mention the incident with that creature yet, but finding out the Sky Lords existed had changed everything. If the Waki'tani were real, then what else might there be in the world? What if all the things I had I passed off as just legends and sage smoke actually walked in the day-to-day world? I wanted to get out there and see it all. It would never happen, though. I wasn't just Siann, I was Grey Lodge, Elder in training. There was no time for exploring or journeying in my life. Matra had trained me to replace her, and everyone knew it. And it was what I wanted, had always wanted, wasn't it? Now the Road was at my feet, and my heart shook like a dog climbing out of deep water.

"Oh Sky Lord," I prayed desperately. *"If you do fly over this village, help me!"*

It had been ages since I thought of myself as a hatchling, but how I wish I could still be one now. I tried hard to grow up, to be responsible. I even stopped spending as much time with the other young girls in the camp. I was afraid their constant talk would make me want things other than the road my mother had set before me.

I couldn't even remember the last time Matra came out berry picking with us, because she was always so busy. So many people needed her advice or the medicines she could make from the roots and leaves of the forest. She was always busy, meeting with the other Elders, teaching the Kit'na; there was never time. Suddenly, it was too much, and there, in the middle of a bramble bush, I sat down and cried until my eyes were red. Thunderclouds started swirling around inside my head, little lightning strikes prickling the back of my eyes. "I can't do it!" I cried to whoever might be listening. "I am not ready to live that life. I don't want to be chained to the lodge and the campfire."

§

A long time later, I heard Mother calling from outside the berry patch, and quickly stifled my sniffles on the sleeve of my tunic. I wasn't fast enough. She pushed her way into the bushes and sat beside me, unexpectedly pulling me onto her lap and cuddling me the way she did when I was a baby. *She smells the same,* I thought, *like campfire and berries and safety.*

"You don't fit in my lap anymore, Little Hawk." Mother smiled sadly. "You've grown, in a lot of ways, this spring."

I hiccupped, rubbing my aching eyes. She hadn't called me Little Hawk for a long time. "I feel trapped, Maskim." I wiped a dirty sleeve over my face, smearing tears and dust all over myself. "I couldn't wait to be a grown-up, but I'm not ready. I don't want to deal with rituals and villagers and mates. The world is so big, and I feel so small."

From beyond the bushes, I heard a quiet peeping. Sticking my head out of the brambles, I watched as a black-and-white storm-skimmer landed in the muck and started digging for bugs. "Look at him, Siann," Mother said kindly. "He is just a small, unassuming bird hunting food in the shallows, but there is no other that flies further or higher into the storm than he does. I know you feel overwhelmed. You are just a hatchling yet. No one expects you to be a skimmer before your wings have grown."

§

Mother left me to calm down and I watched the skimmer for what felt like ages before I picked up my tattered dignity and headed home. I was halfway down the gully when I saw the brush ahead twitch and sway. Something was moving.

It was coming through the forest from the direction where I had seen the Sky Lord early in the spring. The trees below me rustled. Whatever it was, it was big. I jumped like a startled partridge when a husky young voice let out a muffled, "Shards!"

What was he doing out here, I grumbled to myself. That dratted Y'keta always gets in my way.

Ever since I stood up for him at the campfire, it felt like he had been trying to put me in my place. Treating me like one of the children. If it weren't for me, he wouldn't be here! I looked down from the height of the ridge and saw Y'keta glance around furtively before he stepped back on the trail and headed to camp. Now where had the annoying weasel been coming from, and why had he been so anxious not to be seen?

Clambering down, I inspected the grass where Y'keta had broken through the underbrush. Just off the path, I could see a flat spot in the grass where I guessed that he had been sitting. Shoving my way through the brush, I entered the clearing. The trees around looked undisturbed and I couldn't see anything on the mulchy ground to betray his purpose. Then, from the corner of my eye, I caught a glimpse of grey sticking out from under a pile of dead leaves. I moved the leaves, careful not to disturb the spiders. There were lots of spiders this year. It was a bunch of feathers—grey, green, red, and one the blue-black of a raven's wing.

The feathers were carefully twined together with a leather band. Was this part of a magic bundle? I know many of the older people kept feathers for good luck, but a raven's quill was a bit odd. Ravens were considered birds of evil omen. I buried the feathers and piled the brush back over them, squeezed through the thick brush, and stepped back onto the trail. That shell-headed Kit'na was up to something! I'd have to keep an eye on him.

A large bird flew overhead, its shadow making me jump. I froze in place for just a moment. Looking up, I saw a raven, dark against the sky. My mind took a huge jump—was this a raven? Or was it the black raven creature I had seen that night on the ridge? Had Y'keta included raven feathers in his bundle to honour the Waki'tani? He didn't seem the religious type. In fact, he was kind of cynical whenever the matter of beliefs or legends came up. Wasn't he the one who laughed at the Legends of the Sky Lords saving the village, even though that legend was one of our oldest and most sacred. By the time I slipped back into the lodge, it was completely dark and the last meal fire had burnt down to embers. So many new things were going around in my mind, not the least of which was suspicion.

Eight

History Lessons

The next morning, Y'keta sat in the Grey Lodge listening to the elders discuss the scrolls of the Waki'tani. They had been going over the manuscripts since noon, and now it was almost dusk. His backside was numb. The muscles in his jaw tightened as he listened to the stories of the last great war with the Utlaak from the villagers' perspective. They described the Waki'tani as almost Gods. Great beings who soared above the earth and had plummeted down from the lightning to save the Village. It was mythical, it was epic…it was untrue.

Y'keta remembered his father's stories of that war. It had been brutal and ugly. So many died, their songs never heard again, their journeys unfinished. His sister, Netta, led the battle flights—her sharp talons tipped with metal, and her spear shining in the bright sun. How he had envied her.

He had slipped out of camp the day before to try and warn Surta that the Utlaak had been burrowing in the area. He should have had scouts in the area, but Y'keta hadn't seen them. All he could do was place a warning near the camp and hope it brought one of the Roost Guards to investigate.

Pulling his attention back to the village, Y'keta tried to focus as Matra read from a scroll describing the tunnels of the Utlaak. Their dark, damp world lit only by the cold glow of a phosphorescent fungus they grew in the caverns. Twisting and turning, always headed down, the tunnels led deep and deeper into the earth. The heat built up until even sweating did not ease the torment. He remembered the beauty in those tunnels from his one forbidden trip underground; the one that ended with Surta taking his wings and sending him here to Esquialt.

Crystals glimmered in the eerie green caverns, bringing a sparkling firefly light to the passages, cold and unwelcoming. A mile under the earth, there was a sharp corner. Y'keta wrapped his wings around himself to squeeze sideways between the jagged rocks. The tight passage opened into an immense cavern. Towers of solid crystal, tall as a pine tree, grew from floor to ceiling. They were almost translucent in the strange green light. Bent and turned at unnatural angles, the great pillars had made him feel a little nauseated. It felt as though the balance of the world, the basic knowledge of up and down, was somehow tilted. White flakes twinkled in the light of the torch he carried. Snow underground. It was beautiful. He had reached a talon into the white billows, astonished when it came away covered with rock crystals, single strands of salt and rock, as delicate as snowflakes, growing like grass in that forsaken place.

Shaking off the memories, he watched Siann fidgeting. She was trying to take notes from what Matra was reading but looked incredibly bored. Y'keta smirked as Matra noticed Siann's expression and fixed a spear-sharp gaze on the annoying hatchling.

"Siann," Matra said, "from the way you are fidgeting around, anyone would think the lodge had a problem with anthills. Are we perhaps reading too slow for you?"

Blushing, Siann settled herself and folded her hands in her lap. "Oh no, Elder, I am just anxious to understand why the Utlaak come. The scrolls say there have been many wars against the under-dwellers. But what are they looking for? They hate the sun," Siann said, "it harms them. They don't need our supplies, there is food for everyone in the forest and ocean."

"An insightful question." Matra commended Siann with a nod. "Does someone want to venture an answer?"

Without thinking, Y'keta gave them the answer Surta had always given him. "They come because they have to come."

Matra frowned. "Explain yourself, Kit'na."

"Forgive me, Elder." He blushed an unbecoming shade of brick under his tan. "I was taught the Utlaak over-breed. They outgrow their burrows and then they cannot contain the young in their tunnels. The last generation comes out to fight against the over-landers, us. The strongest survive, returning to the burrows. The weak and infirm die; the colonies improve."

"Interesting," Matra said. "A good idea, and it could be true. However, if it is so, why do those who come out of the tunnels appear to be fully grown? I don't recall any record of young attacking the surface."

Y'keta looked at the scuffed dirt floor of the lodge, ignoring Siann's smirk at him from behind Matra's back. Drat the girl. She had a way of making him feel like a hatchling still missing his pin feathers. It reminded him so much of Netta—always thinking, always planning. Siann never seemed to just act; everything was weighed and measured.

"Siann!" Her sniggering look at Y'keta had caught Matra's eye. "Exactly what do you find so amusing? Y'keta proposed a valid explanation for the cycle of wars. It is a good idea and may be plausible. I haven't heard you suggest anything."

Y'keta looked at Matra, his plain face with its sharp features and hooked nose glowing at her recognition. "Yes, Siann," he asked politely. "What is your theory? Why do they come? You must have considered this, being such a thoughtful person."

Siann stood up and picked a few loose twigs from her tunic. "I think they come because they can. Not because of any pressure on resources in the tunnels, just because after the wars, we forget. We stop looking for them. They creep a small way forward; we allow it. They advance another step; we allow it. Until finally they grow brave enough to start again."

"It still doesn't answer your own question," Y'keta asked. "What do they seek to gain?"

Siann's bright eyes grew quiet and considering. "I don't know. I think if we did know we could stop this cycle and maybe never have an Utlaak war again. Has anyone ever asked them? Tried to speak with them?" Siann looked inquisitively at the assembled Shaman. "They have to be somewhat intelligent to tunnel, and organised to raid."

"Who would speak to such creatures." Y'keta's voice rose angrily thinking of Netta's pretty, blue wings shredded and still. "They torture their prisoners, take the eyes from the dead. They are beyond anything decent and good."

"But the young one poses a real question," D'vhan spoke up from where he had been dozing against one of the lodge poles. "Has anyone ever talked to the Utlaak? Can we try? I am willing to attempt something foolish to make it happen, if there is a chance of preventing so much death on both sides."

The entire lodge gasped.

"D'vhan!" Matra's voice was more strident than Y'keta had ever heard it as she glared down at the indolent Warrior Leader. "You will not try this! I will lose none of my children, even those old enough to know better, on such a foolhardy adventure."

D'vhan shook back his coarse red hair, sending the beads woven through it dancing wildly. He sank down against the thick wooden pole of the Grey Lodge and stretched out his long legs unconcernedly. "It's an idea." He shrugged mildly. "All ideas are worth consideration." There was a crafty look on D'vhan's face—his eyes too wide, smile just a touch too careless—that made Y'keta think considering the idea might not be all D'vhan was planning to do.

The summer sun made Y'keta blink as he stepped out of the Grey Lodge. His boots kicking up the mix of dust and dry needles that lay around the central campfire, he hurried after D'vhan. "What are you up to, D'vhan?"
D'vhan darted a mischievous smile at Y'keta, ducked into the Red Lodge, and started idly fidgeting around with the supplies the Lodge kept for hunting trips. "I'm tidying up," his deep voice rasped like gravel as he tied up a thick bundle of hides with some old leather thongs. "Something I wish you and the other lazy Reds would do now and again!"

"D'vhan," Y'keta said, "I'm not some Grey fool with a mind bemused by sage smoke and ceremony. You are planning a trip to the Barrow to try to contact the Utlaak." Thunderclouds swirled in his stomach. Y'keta reached out and touched D'vhan's shoulder, making the warrior jump and fall cursing into the stack of arrows leaning against the lodge wall.

"What on earth was so sharding important that you had to startle an old man! I should take you out and have you whipped." Gnarled muscles flexed under D'vhan's tight-fitting black tunic as he picked up the tumbled pile of arrows. Each movement was controlled and precise, hardly the actions of someone who could be startled by anything, much less an insignificant Kit'na.

"You can't go down the burrows, D'vhan." Y'keta's mind was buzzing like an up-ended beehive. How could he convince D'vhan without saying too much? The old warrior was far from slow and there was already that annoying hatchling sniffing around at everything he did. "We had a barrow near my village. People who went in never came out!" There, that was true, or close enough to true.

"I'm not going into the barrow, Hatchling." D'vhan looked at him, his grey eyes distant and cool. "But someone has to find out why this war never ends, or we go on cycle after cycle sending our best young warriors onto the Road too soon." D'vhan stepped out of the lodge and marched across the camp to the Grey Lodge. Unfortunately, having to weave between the young Green Feathers who raced around camp, running over the slower-moving elders like charging baby buffalo as they played, kind of spoiled the effect.

Traipsing after the swiftly moving Red leader, Y'keta tried to think of something he could say to keep D'vhan from going. He could explain what the burrows were like, let D'vhan know he had been inside one, but they would want to know when and where, and he couldn't tell them.

D'vhan marched into the Grey Lodge and stalked over to where Matra was still sitting with Siann and the other Greys looking at the maps Laban had brought from Atiskaat. "I'm going to try," he said. His head was high, mouth set in a slash across his weathered face. He was not asking permission.

Matra's eyes flashed as she stood up, pulling herself to her full height and authority. "Red Lodge is forbidden!"

"Red Lodge is not going," D'vhan said. "I am going. Just one old crow with cycles of experience in dealing with enemies. No real loss to the village if something goes wrong." D'vhan looked around the assembled Greys. Most were older than him with years of service and knowledge in their heads. "Red Lodge is not Grey. We do not become more as we age; we become less. I will not step onto the Sky Road knowing my warriors fight and die in a war I did not try to stop."

"You are wrong." Y'keta blurted the words out before Matra could contradict D'vhan. "I have seen the burrows near my village. I have been inside them. This task doesn't require experience. It needs someone who can fit down the tunnels and who is fast enough to get out if the Utlaak are still there."

D'vhan's shoulders snapped back and he snarled at Y'keta. "I told you, I do not plan to go down the barrow, just to observe the behaviour of the Utlaak from outside."

Matra collapsed on a pile of hides. Wrapping her arms around her stomach, she laughed until tears rolled down her face. Hooting merrily, she pointed an unsteady finger at D'vhan. It took a moment for coherent words to come out, and she was still chuckling to herself when she spoke. "In all the years I've known you, D'vhan, you never have. Ever. 'Just sat outside and watched.' If there is a tunnel, you go down it. If there is a tree, you go up it."

D'vhan harrumphed.

"I will go," Y'keta offered. "D'vhan can instruct me on what to watch for and how to deal with any enemies I see." He turned to Matra, pulling his shoulders and his tunic straight. He met her eyes with a focused intensity uncommon for the young warrior. "When we fought the Utlaak at Atiskaat, I was your eyes. Let me be so again." Y'keta's fists clenched and unclenched as he waited for Matra's decision.

"You won't stay away, D'vhan, so I will not tell you to stay here." Matra's eyes were still twinkling but her manner became increasingly more purposeful, and it was as Salixt she spoke next. "We will take a party down the coast. Y'keta, D'vhan, myself, and two other warriors." She idly traced along the map from the coast to where the river poured out from the north. "At the river mouth, Y'keta, you will travel north to the barrow and investigate. You will do only what D'vhan instructs. No exploring, no chances."

Matra stepped so close to D'vhan that they stood almost nose to chest-bone. She pointed a wrinkled finger at his solemn face. "We will establish a base at the river mouth, and then we will travel into Atiskaat to check on Siamaat. I am worried. Losing four of her children may have unbalanced her, and she, at least, knows you. We may need to evacuate Atiskaat if there is a real threat, and their leader will need to be ready. We will return to the camp at the river within three days."

Matra turned her intense glare on Y'keta, although she didn't feel it necessary to physically intimidate the younger warrior. "Whether you have seen any signs of Utlaak or not, you will return to the river camp at the end of those three days. If you have seen activity, you will report it. I will then set safe limits for you and D'vhan to investigate it together."

Matra raised her hand towards the great eagle carving hanging in the centre of the lodge. Light seemed to jump from the smoke hole at the top of the lodge, outline the eagle in blinding white, then descend to surround Matra. The flickering lights danced around her engulfing her in swirling green and blue, like the Northern Dancers in the winter dark. "Sky Lords, we seek your blessing on this venture. Give us wisdom and good fortune." Dropping her hand, she stretched wearily. "We will leave in three days. D'vhan, Y'keta, go and prepare your warriors."

As the two Red Feathers left, Matra turned to Siann, who was sitting against the hide wall of the lodge. "Daughter, please go and gather the Grey Feathers, and bring Laban of Atiskaat. There is something we must do before I leave."

Nine

Walking the Lightning
<<<Siann>>>

Y'keta held the thick hide flap open for D'vhan and hurried after him. I gave myself two deep breaths to enjoy the fact that he was gone, then headed out to find everyone Mother had asked for. Laban was easiest to find. He was talking to Ren and Pey't outside the Green Lodge. I waved at him and pointed to the Lodge. He nodded, said something to Ren that made her fidget uncomfortably, and then headed briskly towards the Grey Lodge.

I caught up with most of the other Shaman by weaving between the smaller family lodges, and then I sent the Green Feathers scurrying to find the few Greys who were not in their tents. My mother was pulling the ceremonial bundles from the rafters as I slid back into the lodge. Picking up an ancient-looking hide, sun-bleached to a brilliant white, she hung it on the bone pegs across the opening of the lodge. I tingled all over. Mother always said I was too young to be included in the ceremonies, even though I was learning the ways of the Grey Feather. Spotting Hahnee's bulky form squatting on the floor, I ducked behind him and sat down, trying to be unobtrusive. There was no way I was going to let mother see me—it would give her a chance to ask me to leave.

Matra stood looking solemnly at the Grey Feathers. "Laban of Atiskaat, would you step outside for just a moment. I need to speak to my children."

Laban frowned, his grey eyes looking confused and a little hurt. "Certainly, Salixt," he said. "I will be just beyond the hide."

Touching his arm as he walked past her to the ceremonial door, Mother gave an apologetic smile. "We won't be long."

Laying the ceremonial bundle in the shadow of the eagle statue, Matra looked around at the gathered Shaman. I noticed with dismay how few of us there were. Laban's mother was ill again and could not join us. Hahnee was here, his placid face glistening with sweat and grease from the cookfire he had been tending when I found him. It made me wonder who he left to prepare the evening meal. Hahnee was a fantastic cook.

Mother looked solemn. "Life is changing, my children," she said as she took her place on the sacred hide stretched out under the great eagle.

I couldn't stand it anymore. "What is changing, Salixt?" I asked, still fearful of being forced to leave.

"You all know I am going to Atiskaat with D'vhan," Matra explained, letting a heavy silence build. "I fear their Mother may be irretrievably damaged by the tragedies Laban reported. If this is true, then we must plan to replace her almost immediately." Matra glanced at the closed door to the lodge. "Laban is wise and has power, and will have more power after he is called to the Lightning. Nevertheless, he is young, and Atiskaat will need someone who can be both shaman and Mother to the village if Siamaat is truly gone."

Matra carefully drew a dark-green medicine stone from the ceremonial bundle and held it up in front of the gathered Shaman. A soft gasp ran around the lodge. This was the Tiamat, the speaking stone of the Elder Stars. Drawing her knife from its sheath, Matra made a shallow slice across her bare arm. Blood ran freely until her palm was stained, and red drops fell on the ceremonial hides.

"Green for our forest, Stone for the mountains we came from, Red for the blood connecting the hearts of the People." Matra's voice echoed in the dim lodge. *She's using her*

Salixt voice, I thought, *I can hear the Lightning in her words.* "Sky Lords, breathe light into this, your creation. Speak to your People. Find for us the heart of Atiskaat."

Walking around the lodge with the stone resting on her bloody palm, Matra stopped in front of each of the elder Grey Feathers in turn. She held the Tiamat out in front of Rallet. No response. She stopped in front of grey-haired Barien. Still no change. The stone remained dark and silent.

Then she paused in front of Savohn. The quiet, reserved shaman had started his life with the warriors, only joining the Grey Lodge on the death of his mate. The stone flashed. A green light beamed from the heart of the stone directly towards his chest.

"Savohn," Matra's voice was filled with the echoes of Thunder. "The Sky Lords have spoken and named you as the heart of Atiskaat. If Siamaat is unable, will you take this upon yourself? Become their heart? Their Mother? Their Father?"

Savohn stared at the floor for what felt like a long time, then looked up with tears in his quiet brown eyes. "Salixt, I pray it is not necessary, but should the call be mine, my heart answers gladly."

I bit my lips and fidgeted madly. I was trying so hard not to be noticed! Could no one else see the problems this would cause? "But Mother," I burst out. "What about Laban? He is counting on returning to Atiskaat when his training is over."

Matra smiled, one of those smug, adult smiles that always reduced my stomach to a tangled ball of frustration. There was nothing I hated more than being talked down to or ignored, which apparently she was going to do.

"One more thing and we will be done." Matra looked relaxed and confident as she paced around the lodge. Whatever this last thing was, she was not nervous about it. "We are too few, and with Savohn leaving for Atiskaat, will be even fewer. I think we need to invite Laban within our circle. His training is almost complete, and he is ready for the trials."

My breath whuffed out in a blast of relief. I thought she was going to ask me to Walk the lightning. The idea terrified me. I wasn't ready, at least not yet.

The mood of the gathering lifted immediately. Laban was well-liked and everyone knew he was only months away from taking the trials in his own village. "Call him in, Siann." Matra laughed. "I think he has fretted long enough."

§

Laban paced back and forth outside the Grey Lodge. He watched Ren as she sat peacefully in the spring sunshine, an oily old piece of hide gliding up and down the curve of her longbow. "It must be easy," he said, somewhat foolishly, "to have a calling that requires only physical strength and courage."

Ren looked at him, her green eyes cool and appraising. "You are nervous," she said, her long-fingered hands never stopping their smooth motion up and down the limbs of the bow.

"How can I know," Laban said. "What could they be doing in there? Why would Matra call me to a ceremonial meeting only to ask me to leave the moment they begin?"

Ren grabbed Laban's strong hand and tugged herself to her feet until she stood looking down on the stocky shaman. "You are ready for whatever demands Matra may place on you."

The ceremonial hide fluttered and Siann stepped out of the lodge. "Matra would like you to step inside, Laban, and to thank you for your patience."

With a quick guilty glance at Siann, Ren dropped Laban's hand and hurried away.

The Shaman sat in a circle around a ceremonial hide at the centre of the dirt floor. Matra stood as he approached, and bowed, honouring him. "Laban, Inkiss' son, Grey Child of Atiskaat, enter the circle." This was the first time anyone had ever called him by his ceremonial name. Just hearing it made Laban's chest puff out and his spine snap straight. His entire history was written in that calling; his name, his mother, his choice to follow the Grey path and the village that opened their hearts to teach him.

Eyes quizzical, he looked at Matra as she stood waiting for him in the circle. It felt like something had changed since he had left a few moments ago. Matra now wore the full ceremonial dress of Salixt; the Red, Grey, and Green beaded cloak. She carried her staff with its ancient carvings of Lightning and Thunder.

Even the air felt stiff with anticipation as Laban returned Matra's bow. "How may I serve you, Salixt of the People?"

"The Lightning has spoken, Laban, once of our village," she said, "and it has called your name."

His face paled, and he shook his head at Matra's words. "I am not ready. I thought it would take until winter before the Lightning spoke my name."

"I know you expected for the ceremony to happen in winter." Matra's voice was serious but not solemn. Her brown eyes looked into his grey ones as equals. "However, I cannot delay with the Utlaak threatening and the conditions in the villages. I want you to Walk the lightning and become shaman. But not for Atiskaat. For this village, for Esquialt."

Laban shook his head in denial. "I am of Atiskaat. Why would you ask me to leave them?" He thought of the people in Atiskaat, those murdered by the Utlaak, their children thronging around him as he walked into the village. He remembered Siamaat's eyes, lost and confused. "My heart is for Atiskaat."

"I do not doubt you, Laban." Matra reached out a conciliatory hand towards him. "But Atiskaat requires more than a shaman. They need a new Mother to support Siamaat until she can be healed. They need someone who can stand as Red Lodge leader until one comes or rises from among them. They also need a shaman."

Light glinted from the ceremonial cape as Matra shrugged helplessly. The small beads made a bright tinkling sound seemingly out of place in the tense atmosphere. "None of the Villages have three people they can send. I have one: Savohn. He was trained as a warrior, his wife was the mother before Iamaat, and he has been my right hand here for the last ten cycles. Atiskaat loves you. They need him."

The Tiamat confirmed it. Matra held the bloody green stone at chest height and walked towards him, but no spark burned in its depths. As soon as she moved towards Savohn, the stone flared bright green, and a pulsing beam shot straight at the chest of the older shaman.

"I would have you here," Matra said, "studying under me not as a Kit'na, but as one of my own. You must choose."

Laban looked at the motes of dust suspended in the still air of the lodge. He took a deep breath, allowing the smell of herbs and warm cedar to cleanse his mind and quiet his racing thoughts. Turning to face Savohn, he bowed formally. Stretching his clenched fists straight out in front of him, he took a slow deep breath and, with tears running down his unlined face, turned his hands over, opening them to release the People of Atiskaat and all his work and dreams for their welfare into Savohn's care.

Eyes red, voice cracking, Laban looked at Matra and said, "I come to serve. If you say I am ready, then I will try."

At his words, a less charged, more ceremonial, atmosphere filled the room. Matra took her place at the centre of the circle and began speaking the ancient words.

"What brings you to us? Why have you come asking to Walk between the People and the Storm? What do you bring that we should allow you to enter in as a shaman?"

"Salixt, I bring no gift, no power or knowledge." Laban spread his arms wide, his unadorned robe falling open to show he carried no weapon or mark of office. "I bring only need;

the need of the people for a shaman, and my need to protect them."

"The Elder Stars are hidden by the Golden Eye of Riad," Matra said. "How should we know you speak the truth?" Matra grasped her staff with both hands. She held it in front of her, as though she would strike Laban with it if his answers did not meet with her approval.

"Let the Lightning try my spirit," Laban spoke solemnly, his grey eyes quiet and accepting. "If it finds me unworthy, I will bear the consequence."

"Enter the Lightning Circle then, son of Atiskaat, and understand—no one who enters leaves unchanged." Stepping into the centre of the circle, Matra lifted the staff over her head and closed her eyes. Lightning flashed through the smoke hole of the lodge, illuminating both the staff and its wielder. With a quick, forceful motion, she planted the rod in the packed soil at the centre of the circle and stepped away. The shaft sparked and shone green and blue as though it held the Northern Dancers trapped in its heart.

Laban removed his robe and, clad only in kaal-hide breeches, walked purposefully into the circle. He paced around the staff three times in the direction of sunrise, then, bowing low, grasped it with his bare hands, and with one smooth pull freed it from the dirt and held it high above his head.

As ripples of power danced through the staff, he became the centre pin in a great wheel of light. Rays burst from the staff through his body and out to all of the Shaman standing in the circle. Blue, green, red, and purest white, the light sprayed out from the tip of Matra's staff through Laban's hands and splashed against the hide walls of the lodge. Mouth open in a silent scream, hands clenched convulsively, Laban shook with the power pouring through him, but his eyes stayed calm and focused. One minute, two minutes, it seemed to go on forever but eventually the light stopped and, bowing, he handed the staff, once again only a piece of wood, back to Matra.

Matra turned to the gathered Shaman. "Brothers and sisters, will you join with me and welcome Laban of Esquialt as one of us, teach and honour him, walk with him on the Lightning Road?"

"We will, Salixt. Let him be shaman among us and let us honour him."

§

As the Shaman trickled out of the Grey Lodge, each came up to Laban with a word of welcome, praise, or encouragement. He returned each handshake with a shaky smile and eyes that shimmered silver, like moonlight on deep water.

Looking around, he saw Ren slipping into their lodge. "Huh," he gently mocked himself. She had agreed to stay with him one night, and already it was *their* lodge. Excusing himself, he walked past the cheering children who had been running around him caught up in their Elder's excitement, and lifted the painted hide flap covering the entrance. Ren was looking at the door as he entered. There was no way to be so quiet she would not hear him.

"You did it," she said solemnly.

"Did you see?" He walked across the lodge to stand in front of her. "Did you hear the Lightning speak to me?"

Ren shook her head and brushed her long fingers down the faded kaal-hide leggings she always wore. "I saw you go into the lodge, and then light flashed on the hides. A few minutes later, Matra came out and announced you were now a shaman, and it was over."

Laban picked up the end of Ren's flaxen braid. "There were lights," he said bemusedly, "green as your eyes, pale as your hair, blue as the sky just before sunset." Absentmindedly twirling Ren's hair around his fingers, he raised it to his lips. "It sounded like warmth and strength and courage. The Lightning sounded like you, Ren. It sounded like you."

Ren's green gaze briefly met his gentle grey eyes, then dropped, finding something terribly important to examine on her fingernails.

Laban tugged gently on her long braid. "Up here, silly." Ren glanced up and was caught in a fire trap—or was it ice? Either way, she couldn't lower her eyes, couldn't come up with anything cutting or sharp, no words to allow her a safe retreat. Laban's large, square hand slid down the side of her face and curved around the sharp point of her chin. "Have courage, Little Hawk, it's only a kiss."

Sliding his hand around the back of her neck, he slowly bent her head down until their lips met. She could have backed away. She was taller and stronger than the solid, squat shaman, but for some reason, her knees wouldn't move. She was trapped. Her cool green eyes full of questions; his full of pale fire and answers. His lips were soft, not hard or demanding, and he held the kiss for only a moment, letting her feel the strength of his hand behind her neck, the warm, tangy flavour of his lips. Then he moved away, and she felt cold, empty in a way she had no words to explain.

Once again, Laban slid his warm hand over her cheek, his thumb skimming over her lips. "Thank you," he whispered.

"What for?" Ren prickled at him, "As you said, it was only a kiss."

Taking her hand and placing it on his tunic, right over his heart, he answered, "It is never 'only a kiss' when it comes from you. From you, every moment, every closeness is a gift, and one I know you do not give lightly."

Ren gulped and turned away. How had this man burrowed so far into her that he could see these things? Maybe he was using his skills as a shaman to see through her?

"Let's go and see if the campfire is ready," she said a bit breathlessly. "Matra may need help preparing for her trip to Atiskaat. Did you give her the map?"

Laban gave a gentle yank on her braid and released her hand, letting her step away from him. "Come on, Little Hawk," he said, "or should I call you Rabbit?"

Ren ducked quickly through the flap of the lodge which Laban was holding open for her. Laughing merrily, he followed her into the sunshine.

Ten

Atiskaat is dead

Three days later, the small party set up camp along the river. Against D'vhan's protests, Y'keta left alone to push through the thick brush towards the barrow they had found in the spring, while he and Matra headed towards Atiskaat taking with them the two young warriors who had come as Matra's bodyguards. It took hours for them to trek up the rocky beach to Atiskaat. Clouds of bugs and the whir of crickets were announcing the coming sunset before they even saw the village.

It was quiet as they stepped off the beach and onto the trail. They should have seen stray dogs chasing the children around, looking for scraps from dinner. There should have been a hum of conversation from the adults gathered around the campfire. But there was nothing. Lights shone through some of the tents, and Matra could see shadows moving, but no one was outside enjoying the mild summer night.

She looked at D'vhan. "No guards? Even without a Red Leader, they should have had someone watching the trails."

"I don't know, Matra," D'vhan said. "When we came here before, there were watchers on every trail." The pine needles crunched underfoot as they stopped beside the dead ashes of the central campfire. D'vhan pointed at the half-burned logs and cracked firestones surrounding the campfire. "This fire hasn't been lit for days, look at the rain water sitting in the pit."

Matra shook her head sadly. "Hail Atiskaat," she said. "Matra of Esquialt Village comes from the Roads."

After a moment's hesitation, and some hushed whispering from the nearest tents, a middle-aged man stepped into the centre of the campsite. "I am Amakil, once of Red Lodge, please come into my tent. We are not to be outside after the sun sets."

Posting the two young warriors to guard the trails in and out of the village, D'vhan and Matra entered Amakil's lodge. Matra cried out in distress as she saw five or six wounded warriors lying stretched out on the floor of the lodge. "What is going on here, Amakil?" Matra seemed to grow taller; you could almost see the lightning and thunderclouds swirling around her head. "Where are your healers? Who is tending these people? This is disgraceful."

The odour of blood permeated the tent, along with the sickly sweet smell of infection. "Siamaat forbade." Amakil shrugged helplessly. "She said no one is to be out of their own lodge after dark, and no one is to go out of the village at any time, whether to hunt or to get fresh herbs for the wounded. It has been like this for almost a week." Amakil dropped his head, fat cheeks flushed with shame. "She is the only Elder we have left, what can we do but obey."

"Where is Siamaat?" D'vhan laid a comforting hand on Amakil's shoulder. "I may be able to reason with her. She knew me once." He sighed softly. "She has been fading for years, Amakil, ever since her daughter died, when I was a Green Feather in this Village. Every year she withdrew a little more from the camp. Even before I left to become Kit'na in Esquialt, she was seldom seen outside the Green Lodge."

"You were here as a child?" Amakil peered at the grizzled warrior leader and shook his head. "I'm sorry, I don't remember you."

D'vhan laughed almost merrily. "You were one of the Green Feathers when I left. My name was Dovhan then," he said. "I became D'vhan when I joined the Red Lodge in Esquialt. Don't worry about remembering, it was many cycles ago."

"She will not leave the Green Lodge," Amakil mourned. "She has been there for almost a week now without eating or drinking. I fear her mind is overthrown."

Matra knelt on the floor between two wounded villagers. "What happened to you, my friends?" she asked.

"Utlaak," a young man with half-healed gashes across his stomach and chest responded breathily. "Siamaat sent us to clean out the barrow. We were overrun."

"She sent Red Lodge into the barrow, without advising Esquialt or asking for help?" Matra shook her head in astonishment.

"There is no Red Lodge here," the youngster answered grimly. "Our warrior leader died in the initial attack before Laban came back. The rest of the warriors perished in the second attempt to clear out the barrow."

Matra looked at the young man in disbelief. "You tried more than once? Without a warrior leader, or any help from the other villages?" She looked around at the half-dozen wounded men and women laid out on the floor or propped against the walls of the tent.

Amakil answered, anger crackling in his high-pitched voice, "Three times we tried. Three times, at the end the Greys and Greens were the only adults left to send. There is no one left now. This village belongs to the dead."

§

Gathering D'vhan up with her eyes, Matra nodded politely at Amakil and strode into the darkness. The Village surrounded a central campfire, as all the dwellings of the People did. Green Lodge in the south, Red in the north, Grey to the east. Matra headed unerringly for the Green Lodge. The ceremonial hide was blocking the door. It didn't stop Matra. With an angry yank, she swept it aside and stormed in, only to stop so abruptly that D'vhan ploughed into her as he entered.

"Sky Lords, have mercy!" Matra's face went grey, then green. She bolted out of the Lodge, almost knocking D'vhan over in her hurry. Turning aside at the lodge entrance, she vomited violently.

D'vhan stared with disbelief. Siamaat lay like a dead bird on the floor of the lodge, a knife clutched in her childlike hand, and a macabre red smile across her throat. Falling to his knees, he gathered her into his arms and cradled her too frail body.

She was the Mother of his youth. She had taught him to read and write, and to accept the path the Sky Lords gave him. If tears fell as he held her, he didn't notice.

Finally, the thunderstorm of grief died down, leaving D'vhan empty. He took the great buffalo hide that was rolled up against the wall of the lodge and reverently wrapped Siamaat in its warmth.

"You were always cold," he said to the birdlike figure swaddled in the thick hide. "At least now, you will not feel the winter winds." Lifting Siamaat's wrapped body into his arms, he stepped slowly out of the lodge and into the darkness. "We have to…"

"I know," Matra said, touching his arm in comfort. "I have called your guards in from the trail. They will attend to Siamaat with all due reverence. We have to tend to her people." Matra repositioned the ceremonial hide across the opening to the Green Lodge and watched as D'vhan handed the tiny bundle to one of his warriors. Then she slowly led him back to Amakil's tent.

"It is Matra and D'vhan," she called at the door. "May we enter?"

Ducking through the small entrance, Matra looked sadly at Amakil and the wounded. "Siamaat has taken the Road," she said. "We arrived too late."

"She took her own life?" Amakil suddenly looked much older. "Now, without an Elder to lead us? This village is truly gone."

D'vhan laid a comforting hand on Amakil's shoulder. "Atiskaat continues," he said. "Matra will send help. We will rebuild." His eyes suddenly regained their sense of purpose, flashing from the injured villagers to the general state of disrepair in the lodge. "For now, it is up to you to care for your injured and keep the Village fed and safe."

Amakil raised tired, sad eyes to his. "I am not an elder," he said, "how should I lead?"

"You may not be an Elder," Matra interjected, grabbing his shoulder and giving him a firm shake that left his pudgy body wobbling. "But you are Atiskaat, and you will not hide in your tent like a frightened child! These are your people and until Savohn arrives, you will do what needs to be done."

Eleven

In the Dark

Y'keta made slow progress towards the cave where the Utlaak had died a few weeks earlier. From the position marked on the Matra's map, it looked like the same barrow the four dead scouts had found. The blackened grass had started to fill in, soon there would be no sign anything had happened here. *No sign*, he thought, *only the memories of blood.*

It was almost nightfall, and the light of the first stars was faintly visible through the purple sky. "I am Y'keta," he announced with a soft, steady voice. "I mean no harm." There was no way of knowing if the Utlaak understood him, or if they could understand anything. He put down the basket of fruit and corn he had carried from the boat, backed off a few yards, and settled in to wait. Dusk fell and the evening birds sang out their surprise at seeing the solid form of a warrior squatting under their tree. Night came, colder than usual for summer, but still tolerable. He rubbed his arms, thinking wistfully about the thick buffalo fur he had left in the canoe.

Midnight. The Elder Stars were twinkling in the sky and Y'keta watched as comets, the Sky Lords' messengers, fell from the Road to perform their tasks on the earth. Still nothing. He woke up just before dawn, stiff and cramped. Rubbing his eyes, he watched a small Utlaak creep out of the shadows of the barrow to poke the basket of food with a long, sharpened stick. He froze in place watching the hunched figure, trying to absorb who and what these strange creatures were. *About time someone tried to learn about them,* he thought.

To the villagers, the Utlaak had always been a story told around the campfire to frighten unruly children, more mist and smoke than anything real.

One of the scaly creatures worked up the courage to grab a cob of corn from the basket. Holding it awkwardly with pudgy malformed fingers it sniffed the food uncertainly. *Well, they don't seem to want our food,* Y'keta pondered. *That one doesn't even know what corn is.*

The Utlaak skittered back into the darkness with an alarmed bleat clutching the corn to his smooth grey hide as a large, muscular Utlaak appeared from the cave. This one was different, it peered warily at the surrounding forest. Dry overlapping scales rippled across his narrow shoulders with every movement and made rustling sounds as he stalked out of the cave mouth. The large Utlaak stood upright, brandishing one of the crystal-set war swords. *This one is a warrior,* Y'keta thought, *the others, the little ones, are scared of him.* This Utlaak understood what the food was, swiping an armful of fruit, bread, and corn from the basket, it glared at the smaller foragers and smashing a few of them aside with calculated cruelty, disappeared with its prize into the depths of the cavern.

The younger ones cowered against the cave walls until the noise of the warriors' departure had faded, then glancing at the cave mouth fearfully crept slowly out to poke at the basket again. Their lumpy grey bodies scrambled over and around each other like camp dogs after a bone. Pushing and shoving each other as they struggled to get near the food. *They might know enough to fear the larger creature,* Y'keta thought, *but he couldn't see anything that proved they were intelligent. No language he could hear or anything he could understand as an organization.*

Seeing the sun had started to purple the night sky and gauging it to be almost dawn, Y'keta decided to show himself, trusting he could run to the boat before the ungainly creatures could reach him. He started humming softly, mimicking the sounds he had heard the Utlaak make and adding in bird song and night sounds from the world around them. The juvenile Utlaak froze, the loud chittering noise silenced. For a few heartbeats all Y'keta could hear was the sound of their scaly skin rubbing against the walls of the cavern. After a few minutes of staring wildly at him, one of the smaller Utlaak seemed to gather the courage to step back into the clearing.

Y'keta ignored the lizard-like creature as it bravely moved one step beyond the cave entrance. It didn't seem to threaten in any way. It just stared. *Maybe they don't speak*, Y'keta thought. *They could be like animals, just acting from fear and hunger. If so, then I may be able to tame them.* The image of him walking into the Village with an Utlaak for a pet made him laugh out loud, scaring the small Utlaak back into hiding.

"Sorry, little ones," he murmured, starting again to hum, to reassure them he meant no harm. "I did not mean to frighten you."

When the sun finally rose, Y'keta packed up the basket, picked up all the scattered food, and went back to the beach where he had pulled the boat ashore. Yawning, he tucked the basket into the shade of the overturned boat and settled down on the ground to sleep the day away. *I'll try again tomorrow night,* he thought.

He had been sitting at the river's edge after a third quiet night of watching the Utlaak grab food from the baskets he left near the cave mouth. Nothing unusual had happened, no sign of the bigger, more aggressive Utlaak, only the little ones, as he had started thinking of them. They seemed like puppies—curious, eager, a bit fearful, but not intentionally dangerous. The big ones were another matter, one that deserved watching. They were aggressive, brutal even with the smaller creatures that came out of the cave.

§

He woke up with a thump. Something had left his head bloody and aching and was dragging him across rocks and gravel into the dark. Bringing him back to wherever this was. He could only assume one of the massive brutes had attacked him.

He was dragged down the tunnels and thrown on the floor in a room full of the larger Utlaak. They hadn't asked him any questions just pounded him over and over with those Star-cursed maces. No way to run, no way to communicate, not even understanding why, Y'keta curled into a ball and endured.

Is this what happened to Netta? Is this what my selfishness condemned her to? He couldn't stand the thought. Maybe Surta had been right to blame him for her death. He should have done his duty and stayed with her, not run off exploring on his own.

The adults seem to finish with their fun, there was no way it was less than that for them. The sibilant hisses as they spurred each other on to more and more violence spoke volumes for their enjoyment of the sport.

Finally, when Y'keta was nothing but a bloody ball on the floor, and not offering enough resistance to be amusing, the adults pulled one of the bigger grubs into the room.

Obviously terrified and reluctant, the smaller creature cowered away as two of the Utlaak placed one of the maces in his hand and pushed him towards Y'keta. The juvenile turned to run back into the tunnels only to be punched and shoved by the circling Utlaak. Swinging the mace wildly it approached Y'keta. It was obviously not trained to fight, and desperately did not want to. Terrified it dropped the weapon and broke for the darkness again, only to be beaten back towards where Y'keta lay on the blood-soaked floor.

The Utlaak tightened the ring around Y'keta until the scared young Utlaak had no where to move. It stood over Y'keta with the mace raised awkwardly in one malformed hand. Its pudgy fingers could hardly grip the handle and its arms shook uncontrollably as it strained to lift the giant mace. The larger Utlaak howled and screeched until the juvenile, almost reluctantly, dropped the mace on Y'keta's leg.

Howling with pain, Y'keta bounced up and shoved the cowering Utlaak back into the circling pack of adults. He picked up the mace and swung it around his head. Light glittered from the crystal shards making rainbow flickers around the cavern. The shaking juvenile backed away only to be shoved towards Y'keta who was twirling at the centre of the cavern, swinging at anything that came near enough to hit.

Without thinking, Y'keta hammered the trembling creature, the force of the blow knocking it to the floor and leaving blackish trails of blood running down its back. The Utlaak shrieked, a sound so high pitched that Y'keta's more sensitive ears rang in protest.

Its watery grey eyes unfocused and scared, the injured Utlaak writhed on the cavern floor. Streaks of ichor glowed greenish black in the eerie cave light as its skin cracked and peeled away in sheets. Y'keta watched horrified as the Utlaak pounced on the bleeding young one, ripping away the shedding skin until it lay unconscious on the cavern floor, Where the warriors had pulled the skin from its broken body the injured Utlaak was shiny, wet with blood and a green-black fluid that seemed to be seeping out of its pores.

The larger Utlaak picked up the unconscious creature roughly and dragged it out of the main cavern leaving the smaller animals to push forward from the darkness.

The smaller grubs rushed past him, every bump and brush of their scaly hide pure agony on his beaten body.

The larger Utlaak had been most thorough. The club the brute swung over and over had shredded every inch of Y'keta's skin until every bone felt bruised and shattered by the embedded crystal shards in the weapon. The shards of crystal in its mace had torn his skin in more places than Y'keta could count, or wanted to.

Leaning against one of the slick walls of the cave he tried to get his bearings. Flickering green light seemed to come from crystals embedded in the cave walls. It wasn't a cheering light, cold and wavering it made his eyes ache for something solid to focus on.

Father would be almost happy to see me here, he thought. *It would prove, again, that he was right. I never listen to anyone.*

§

There is a point at which pain ends; it becomes part of the background noise of life, no more present than a cricket in the rush floors of the lodge, or the sound of your own heartbeat.

Y'keta no longer thought about pain or darkness, the way he never thought about air as something that existed apart from himself, it simply was. It must have been days now, he thought, or nights. It was always night in here.

"Water," he croaked, more to hear a voice in the chittering silence than in any realistic hope water or food would come. It hadn't so far. "I need water."

Y'keta wasn't sure why he was still alive. Some stubborn piece of his soul refused to step on the Road before him. "I have to live to tell the village," he told himself over and over again. "I have to live."

A brutally bright light assaulted Y'keta's eyes. He curled into a ball, protecting his head with his hands. Light usually meant the older Utlaak were coming, meant more beatings.

"Y'keta—is it you?" It was a deep voice, no longer young, but still one he had never thought to hear again.

"D'vhan," he said, struggling to croak out the words, "how are—why are you here?"

"To retrieve you, foolish child," D'vhan laughed. "Although there almost isn't enough left of you to save." As gentle as a mother with an ailing child, D'vhan picked Y'keta up and started carrying him up the twists and turns of the tunnel. "We have been searching ever since you missed your return to the village. Matra insisted."

After an uncertain time, when every false step or brush against the wall of the tunnel brought sharp jabs of crystal pain, they emerged into a starlit night. The Sky Road shone above him in all its glory, and the Elder Stars looked down as their tired, aching son wept in joy.

As soon as they reached the clearing in front of the barrow, D'vhan laid him gently on a pile of soft furs, which had been tied across a triangle frame of wood. A litter, Y'keta thought. They expected to drag me along like an old woman. He felt himself struggling to breathe, every inch of his skin burning and scarred. They are more right than they can possibly know. I don't think I could stand if the Sky Lords themselves commanded me to.

§

The journey back to Esquialt seemed to take forever. Y'keta lay in the bottom of one of the boats, too weak to sit. After the endless time he'd spent in the tunnels, the morning sunlight torched every exposed inch of skin. His eyes burned even through the dark cloth D'vhan covered his eyes with to protect his vision. Finally, they decided to pull onto the beach and move Y'keta into the shade. They would make camp here and travel home by moonlight.

"How long?" Y'keta's voice, normally loud and piercing, sounded weak. He sipped at the water Pey't passed to him, his lips cracked and bleeding.

"Two moons since you were overdue," D'vhan growled. "We found the barrow three days ago and have been clearing inwards looking for you ever since." D'vhan gestured at the three or four warriors who sat around the makeshift camp quietly tending their wounds. "The Utlaak didn't want to give up their favourite toy."

Y'keta couldn't believe it. "You shouldn't have come," he croaked. "You shouldn't be putting lives at risk for a foolish child."

D'vhan chuckled at the unfamiliar growl in Y'keta's weak voice. Whatever the Utlaak had done, they had not broken him, and may have been the saving of him. "Matra thought you would say something like that. She gave me an answer for you."

Y'keta's eyebrow tried to hide in his filthy blond hair. "Oh, and what did she say?"

"She told me to pass this on exactly." D'vhan's voice went to a higher pitch and took up Matra's sing-song lilt, "Shut up, child. We walk the Road together. No one of the People walks alone."

Y'keta wheezed and coughed, his fluid-filled lungs trying to strangle his breath. The warriors crowded around him, worrying. Nevertheless, Pey't sat back with a huge smile on his fat face. "He's trying to laugh." He chortled, then grunted as he inadvertently jostled his wounded leg. "Not well, but he's laughing."

They arrived in Esquialt on the second night. The slow, easy travelling gave Y'keta a chance to regain a little strength. The gentle light of the moon was no longer attacking his eyes when he removed the blindfold. Matra, Siann, and all the other elders and warriors waited on the shore, reaching out to pull the boats onto the rocky beach.

"How did they know when we would arrive?" Y'keta asked.

"I've sent runners ahead each time we camped," D'vhan explained. "The village was with us every step along the way."

More than the villagers, all of whom were considered his family, Y'keta's heart broke to see the warriors, his brothers and sisters, standing at the water's edge waiting for him. Maybe I'm not quite finished with this Road yet, he thought. Esquialt still has a place for me.

Lifting the frame carefully so Y'keta's battered limbs would not be jostled, the warriors carried him into the Healer's Lodge. For the first time Y'keta could recall, the lodge door was left open—allowing all the villagers to come and see him.

"Now, Hatchling," Sawiea's voice took on a brusque note, making Y'keta think the warm welcomes of a moment ago had been a hallucination. "You need to talk to Matra, and then these people need to leave you alone to sleep."

Twelve

Healers' Lodge
<<< Siann >>>

I stepped into the Healer's Lodge and started to cough, the roof of my mouth felt oily and raw from the acrid smoke drifting up from the leaves Matra threw in the brazier. The mixture of healing herbs and pungent peppermint made my nose twitch.

The warm darkness of the lodge seemed almost womblike, silent except for the feeble moans of the wounded warriors and the crackle of the smudge fire. Within minutes my long hair hung in a damp braid down my back and I was picking at my tunic. It felt really uncomfortable, stuck to me from the sweat running down between my breasts.

Touching Y'keta's face was like touching one of the rocks they used in winter camps, so hot my hand felt burned. His face was ashen. I was surprised my fingers didn't come away from his forehead covered in charcoal. The hide flap that covered the lodge entrance in inclement weather was pulled back, and D'vhan and Sawiea entered, talking quietly. Nodding at me, Sawiea headed to the other side of the lodge, suddenly busy with her own affairs.

"How is he doing," D'vhan asked, bending over the feverish warrior. The day after Y'keta returned to the village a fever had taken him. He made random clicking and whistling noises, but he didn't seem to know anyone or respond to voices. If this was a fever dream, it was like none the healers had never seen.

"Surta!" Y'keta yelled, bolting upright. "A'ta, no!" Then, just like he had all the last times, Y'keta fell back into his delirium.

"Who is Surta?" I asked. It isn't a name I'd heard anywhere before.

"I'm not sure." D'vhan's hard face softened as he wiped Y'keta's feverish brow with a cloth soaked in an infusion of cooling mint leaves. "It must be someone from his home village."

I bent over Pey't, "Didn't anyone tell you to dodge, old crow?" I teased gently. "Now, Uncle Pey't, would you have me believe all those war stories and battle songs you taught me as a child were just exaggerations?"

Pey't attempted a smile as a red-hot cloth soaked in herbs and oils softened and then painfully removed the crusted scab on the portly

warriors' leg. "You're tutting like a partridge."
He gasped with a faint smile.

Moving as quickly as I could, I repacked the
wound with moss and mustard weed and bound
it tightly with clean linen. "Mother will need to
look at this tomorrow, Pey't. I think it's getting
better, but I'm not sure. Until you see her, you
sit here!"

Pey't muttered something about his own bed
and me being a bossy little hawk, but it didn't
work. I just stuck my tongue out and turned
away to look at the young warrior beside him.

With all the wounds checked and the
warriors as comfortable as possible, I nodded at
D'vhan, who was still hovering over Y'keta. "A
few deep breaths of fresh air would help those
in the tent," I said. "Once they have finished
with the smudge fire, roll up one of the side
hides and let the air blow through for a few
minutes, just put extra blankets on those with
fever, especially Y'keta."

"What do you think is wrong with him?"
D'vhan asked, shoving a hand through his
coarse red hair. "He seemed alert enough for
most of the journey back from Atiskaat, then he
just faded."

"Matra will check him in the morning," I
answered. "I'm not as experienced as she is, but
it feels like a shock to his mind more than to his
body. He has been severely beaten, though."

"Obviously so," D'vhan agreed, "every rib was broken, and he will have scars. We can't prevent that. But it's not on the outside where he needs this time to heal. Sometimes I believe the mind needs to be silent to heal, and I think that may be what Y'keta is doing. His body is sleeping to allow his mind to heal."

D'vhan nodded, thinking of his own wounds and the secrets they kept. "Wounds in the mind cannot be healed with herbs and a bandage."

I shrugged, remembering Matra's advice that pretending to know could be worse than admitting ignorance. "I don't know D'vhan." Wiping the sweat from my eyes I got up to leave the lodge. "I just don't feel Y'keta, even though he's lying in front of us. We'll just have to give him time and hope his mind returns."

AUTUMN

Thirteen

Too Much Open Sky
<<Siann>>

The People were moving to the prairies for the autumn hunt. Tents had come down at sunrise with much grunting, groaning, and complaining from the Green and Grey Feathers who had to carry the rolled-up hides. Since I didn't have a tent to fold or a family to pack up, I had the job of emptying out the scrolls from Grey Lodge. I carefully packed up all the manuscripts, giving them a lot more respect than I would have earlier in the spring, and took them to Matra and Laban for transport.

Before the hide walls were untied and the Grey Lodge opened to the sky, Matra had entered alone. She came out a few moments later carrying an ungainly shape wrapped in a white blanket. I knew what it was. Only Mother could take the eagle carving from the roof of the lodge, the one which was inlaid with crystal and focused the lightning when we held ceremonies.

Finally, everything was ready. The village didn't move quickly, or quietly, but it moved. D'vhan went in front with three of his best scouts. Matra and the Grey Feathers walked a few minutes behind, and just behind them were Iamaat, the Greens, the children, and anyone who was not healthy enough to keep pace with the front groups.

The mountains rose up like knives in front of us, topped with their bone-white blades of cloud and snow. They had always fascinated me. I remember Mother telling me tales of the Waki'tani, who lived in the mountains and flew among those clouds. And of course, now that I knew those stories were real, I couldn't get away from the group to explore. I had to watch my baby brother.

"Napaay! Will you please get out of those berry bushes! Napaay, stop tormenting the dogs! Napaay, please don't walk so near the edge!"

"Stars," I mumbled to myself, "I'm going to push him off a ledge before we get past these mountains, I truly am!" Even though I was technically still babysitting, I walked with the Grey Feathers this year. Mother had argued that I should stay further behind, to offer a better chance for one of the Salixt's bloodline to survive if there was a rockslide or other calamity on the narrow ledges. But I insisted. I was carrying a full load of scrolls and firewood like the other Greys, I didn't belong back with the Greens.

We had walked all morning. From my place at the back of the Greys the noise was overwhelming, so was the smell. A brown dust cloud dirtied the sky wherever the people passed, created by the sweat and dust of so many people trampling across the crumbling ledges and through the muddy ravines. By mid-morning, my head was killing me. The sun was pushing knives into my eyes and every footfall sent arrows into my aching head; we could not stop for the afternoon meal soon enough.

I grabbed Napaay from the edge of the ravine for what felt like the fiftieth time. "Go walk with the Greens," I said, "or I'll tell Mother who spoiled her new tunic." There wasn't much those berry-stained fingers didn't get hold of. I knew the threat, even without proof, would be enough to put fear in his eyes. I shoved him down the slope towards the other Greens travelling in a noisy herd in the middle of the column behind me.

With a spiteful glare, Napaay raced backed to Varas, who was shepherding the Green group. "Siann says I have to travel with you." He wrinkled his nose at me. "She doesn't want to walk with me!" His little face fell and artful tears traced through the dust on his pudgy cheeks.

"A deep breath, and another one, he's just a child," Varas whispered as he stepped up beside me. "He just wants attention and is feeling a bit ignored."

I grinned at the fine-featured Green Kit'na. "He's a Geeshoo who doesn't do anything but eat berries and tie up my time."

"Were you any different at his age? Or even at this age? We all need to be significant to someone."

My face must have warned Varas I was in no mood for lecturing because he dropped back to the middle of the Green pack and started to sing one of the children's songs from his village.

High Plains marching to the Buffalo home,
High Plains traveling to where they roam,
Buffalo tongue and sweet hot tea,
Traders tales and toys for me!

He soon had all the children in a marching line, swinging their arms in time as they clambered up and down the rocky trail towards the top of Eagle's Pass. We would hopefully reach the pass by nightfall, camp at the foot of the pass, and in the morning climb to the high plateau.

As we wound through the rising trails, I looked back at the forest far below. I couldn't see the village, but I guessed where it was. As I looked down the mountain trail, I could see the large bay just north of where our canoes were now stored and covered with hides, protected from the wind.

Glancing furtively at the clear sky above me, I shuddered; still blue, still bright, still painful. Dropping my eyes to the rocky trail, I picked my way along a crumbling ledge and was surprised when my feet wobbled a little trying to find purchase on the loose rock. Looking at the scree below my feet, I spotted something glinting at me; a crystal, pink, almost white and about the size of my thumb. Grabbing it quickly, I shoved it in my tunic sleeves. Superstition says crystals are unlucky, but I have always liked them.

Later, after we made camp and rolled into our bed-furs around the fire, I took out the crystal and polished it carefully. Sometimes crystals had sharp edges, they could cut and were likely to infect, but this one was a smooth oval. It felt strange in my hand. I could almost feel a vibration flowing through the stone and into my bones, calming and reassuring me.

It took three days of slow, cautious travel for the village to reach the hunting grounds. The high prairies opened up in front of us. It made me feel funny—few trees, no hills, nothing but the tall prairie grass and the blue sky. *And whatever that was*, I added to myself, staring at a dark spot overhead. This was the third time I'd seen something flying over us. It was at the limit of my sight, but it was there. Too far away to identify as a bird, but birdlike, and big. A bit nervous, I hurried to keep up with the rest of the Grey Lodge.

Thankfully, Napaay had asked to travel with Varas today. He enjoyed listening to the tales of Varas' village and was just as happy not to be tied to his big sister's laces.

The plain felt empty. I should have seen a fox, a herd of kaal dashing away at the noise of our passing, small skimmer birds or partridges poking about in the waving grass. Even so, I heard nothing, saw nothing except the occasional sighting of the strange bird flying overhead. It wasn't reassuring. I hated the trip to the Autumn Camp this cycle.

Fourteen

Siann's Suspicions

Finally, they reached the plains. The grass and stunted trees gave so much less space for an enemy to hide, or an Elder to trip, or a child to wander off unseen. Only now could Y'keta's guard finally drop and his shoulders start to relax.

Falling back to walk companionably beside Ren, who was a rear guard at the moment, he took a few minutes to just breathe in the open air. The air in the forest always smelled—not bad, but potent. The ever-present scent of the pine trees and hundreds of years of mulch carpeting the forest floor was absent here.

Y'keta rubbed his arms, fighting the need to soar was harder here. He felt the air currents and the wind, and his arms prickled with the need to extend his feathers and be gone. Taking several deep breaths to control himself, he reached over and lifted a big bundle of firewood from one of the elders. "In your place, Grandmother," he offered, hiking the bundle over his shoulder.

The old woman gave him a grateful smile, one pointy brown tooth still showing in her wrinkled face. "I thank you, Y'keta." She panted huskily, her arms wrapped around her chest. "I fear this may be my last summer on the plains but killing myself getting to camp was not my plan."

In mid-afternoon, Matra called a halt and a travel camp was set up. Makeshift lodges were erected from wooden poles and kaal-hides. Campfires were started using twigs the children gathered along the way. Y'keta noticed Siann's slumping shoulders. Her usually smiling face was drooping and her ever-inquisitive questions, so often annoying, were silent. Somehow he missed them.

"So Hatchling, have you survived your first trek? It makes a big difference not walking with the Green Feathers, doesn't it?" His tone was deliberately provoking, but there was no sign of her normal retort.

Siann walked with the adults this cycle, carrying a full load of food and firewood as well as her share of the scrolls and trappings from the Grey Lodge. Her small frame had looked twisted under the heavy load, but she held up proudly, never once asking for help.

"I'm worried, Y'keta," Siann whispered. "I don't trust the openness of the plain this year; it feels like something is watching us."

This wasn't at all what Y'keta expected. His conversations with Siann were usually no more than polite disagreements. On a few less-than-mature occasions, they even descended into verbal mudslinging. Y'keta stepped away from the fire just enough to allow his eyes to focus on Siann's tired face. "What do you mean, Siann?" He glanced around for D'vhan, wondering if he should call him over. Was this something the warrior leader should know about?

"That's the problem," Siann grumbled. "I don't know what I mean. I've felt uneasy on this trip in a way I've never felt on the plain before. Things are off balance. The birds are too quiet, and even though we've walked through half of their grazing lands, I haven't seen a kaal yet."

Siann's hands fidgeted nervously with the long braid hanging over her shoulder. "And…. you'll think me foolish," she said, glancing at Y'keta, shrugging helplessly, "but I think an eagle is following us. I've seen him overhead since we left the village, I swear it's the same bird!"

"Have you told Matra," Y'keta said, "or D'vhan?" This might be just nerves because of the attacks at Atiskaat, but maybe Siann had seen or felt something the Elders were too busy to notice.

"No." Siann sighed with hard-won resignation. "I am a hatchling, even you said so. If they do not see the danger, and I can't give them any details, how can I convince them it's real?"

Y'keta thought hard and fast; an eagle might just be an eagle, but then again, it could be one of Surta's scouts following the move. *Especially,* he thought, *if Father received the last message I sent.*

§

Soon after they had returned from the first trip to Atiskaat, Y'keta had announced he was going for a walk. His excuse was a need to practice the trail craft that D'vhan was teaching him. It took him most of the day to find a Kejai, and most of the leather from his breeches and the skin from his knees to catch it. But it had to be a Kejai, the small forest bird had iridescent green feathers almost the same colour as his own feathers in Waki'tani form.

Carefully removing a tail feather from the frightened bird, he had walked into a clearing near the camp and let the bird go. Writing a short warning about Utlaak activity, he tied the note to the feather's shaft.

Scrambling up the tallest tree near the clearing was hard work, but he had done it. He left the message and the vivid green feather fastened to the topmost branch of the tree with a scrap torn from the edge of his tunic, and then climbed down and returned to camp empty-handed. He was more than willing to be called a bad hunter for the chance to warn his father of enemies stirring nearby.

"I don't know," he said truthfully, "I've never been here on the plain before, so I'm not sure what is or isn't wrong. Even so, with the recent attacks, I don't think taking chances is smart."

For once when he looked at Siann, he didn't see an annoying hatchling. Her hair was messy and her boots worn thin from the unaccustomed days of travel, but her face was drawn tight with worry and her eyes met his seriously, without a hint of their normal rancour.

"I'm telling D'vhan," he said, "we'll let him decide if this is something or nothing. I don't know, and if you are honest, neither do you."

Siann shrugged and turned back to the campfire, not noticing the concern on Y'keta's face as his eyes followed her. "Probably nothing," she said, dismissing herself.

Y'keta remembered the night he arrived at the village. She'd tried so hard to look brave, stepping into the firelight and speaking up during the ceremony to welcome the Kit'na. She was just a walker, dirt bound, and yet she stood in front of her own council, even her mother, to defend him. Y'keta thought of his father, who, like Siann's mother, was an Elder of his people. Surta was a formidable person in his own right, but when he stood under the Elder Stars, bathed in clouds with the wild light flickering on his wings, no one, *no one*, stood up to Surta.

No, Y'keta wouldn't dismiss her again.

Surta had been right, he admitted to himself. *As much as I fought coming to the village, I have grown here.* His cheeks burned as he thought of the brash young shell-head Surta had exiled months before. *"But A'ta!" The grey-green feathers on Y'keta's neck ruffled and he sniffed with disdain, "they are just so, so earthbound... what could I possibly learn from them!" Surta looked at his son with a mischievous twinkle in his ancient black eyes. "That, my young hatchling, is the question."*

"You know that our clan has the responsibility of watching over these lands. The Utlaak are never far away."

The wind felt cool as it whispered across Y'keta's wings, the sun bright and the sky cloudless. This is where I belong, he thought resentfully, not down there with the walkers!

Y'keta circled above the village, high enough that he would be taken for an eagle or an osprey if anyone bothered to look up at all, but no one ever did, he scoffed. "The villagers never look up, feet of mud, heads of mud "

"You have flown alone too long my son, and I think it will serve you well to learn to live outside of yourself." Surta looked at his son with a strange mixture of sorrow and anticipation. "When your time is over you can return. But for now, there is much to learn, if only you can convince yourself that you do not already know it all. Now, Prepare"

With a last resentful flip of his feathers, Y'keta settled on the ground beside his father. His feathers shone iridescent green in the forest shadows and a small light of rebellion danced in his yellow eyes. He spread his wings wide, feeling the electricity gather and allowing the sense of power to flow through him. Then, with a resigned droop of his head he – folded-himself inward, creating a small quiet part of his mind where Y'keta lived as a Waki'tani and allowed the rest of his active mind to be filled with the things he would need to live in the walker's world.

Surta spoke and the air seemed to charge with the violence of a thousand thunderbolts, lightning flashed and Y'keta was momentarily blinded. When his eyes cleared, he was unmade. His hands, Hands- where his beautiful black talons had been, slowly moved to the fastening of the cape he was now wearing. A cape of iridescent green feathers that he removed sulkily and placed on the ground before his father. Suddenly Surta reached out with his beak and plucked the raven feather helm from Y'keta's head, leaving him with nothing but a breechclout and a panicked expression.

Picking the robe of feathers up in one powerful Talon, Surta leapt for the sky. 'But what can I do A'ta", Where do I go!".

"Walk, and learn", Surta's voice echoed in his mind. "I will be here should you need me."

Fifteen

Warning the Roost

The next morning, Y'keta paced at the back of the column beside Ren, his mind full of confusion. Siann's concerns aside, it looked like Surta had guards following the People as they wandered the high prairie. Why would he do that? Y'keta could almost feel his crest rising as the old insecure anger reared its head. *He doesn't think I can handle myself without his supervision,* the old resentment swirled through his mind. *He still doesn't trust me.*

Taking a deep breath, he smiled at Ren, who seemed somewhat quiet, even for Ren. Y'keta jumped as she tripped over a root and almost bumped him off the path. Far from watching the trail or keeping an eye out behind them, her green eyes hadn't moved from a certain shaman who was, at the moment, discussing something with Matra and the Greys.

Y'keta hip-checked Ren hard enough to make her step awkwardly off the path. "Pay attention," he said. "Don't expect me to keep the watch for you!"

Ren's eyes flashed dangerously, but she soon went back to scanning the surrounding area.

"I need to slow down a bit," Y'keta dissembled. "I'm still not up to par from Atiskaat. Why don't you move forward and scan along the outskirts of the group, then join up with D'vhan at the front."

Ren's cold green eyes drifted over him with hastily veiled concern. "Are you all right to take the rear alone?"

"The noise and bustle of the group are a bit much for me. Back here I'll be all right. If I need anything, I'll use one of the Greens as a runner." It wasn't untrue, he thought.

It was taking much longer to get used to being back in the village than he had expected. Only a miracle of the Elder Stars had made it possible for the Warriors to rescue him, but after two moons in the tunnels with his only contact either the mindless young Utlaak or their brutal overlords. Y'keta still found he flinched when people came too near him or when voices got too loud.

As Ren pulled ahead of the slow-moving Green Lodge, Y'keta allowed himself to drop back a few paces. Just far enough that he could think without the constant distraction of dust and noise, but not so far that he couldn't catch up quickly if he were needed. No one was watching, so Y'keta reached into his pack and removed a wrapped black feather. Pulling a red bead from his hair, he slid the shaft of the feather through the bead and tied it off with a small piece of cloth. Checking on the column of slow-moving villagers now a good distance in front of him, he quickly left the trail and pushed through the sparse vegetation until he came to a rocky hillside overlooking the trail. A scraggly pine tree was struggling to hold on at the top of the outcropping, fighting against an almost constant wind.

Y'keta leapt up the tree and scampering as high as he could, reaching out to one of the small overhanging branches. Using a piece of leather torn from his vest as a strap, he tied the black raven feather with its red bead to the branch. If his father had scouts nearby, they would see this, and Surta would know there was a danger in the area. Y'keta dared not say anything clearer.

§

The mountains were taunting him. Y'keta grumbled as he watched the slow column of villagers climb like a snake from the forest trails through the pass that led to the high prairies. He could imagine the cold wind in his feathers and the freedom of soaring up and above all this slogging. True, he was stronger after these months with the villagers, but there would always be a part of him resentful of the plodding pace which was the best the ground could offer.

What harm would it cause if the People knew the truth about the Waki'tani? He'd wondered before he joined the Village. Now he knew. The People built their whole world around the mythical presence of the Waki'tani. Finding out they were not gods, just different, would tear the fabric of the Village society into bloody pieces.

§

It took three days to get from the winter village to the hunting camp. Days that would have been moments to him before, but finally Y'keta stood looking down at the caterpillar of People winding its way down the steep incline to the foot of the jump.

It's so much harder here, he complained to himself. D'vhan was worrying over the possibility of an attack from the Utlaak or anything that would call the warriors away before the Elders and the camp were resettled. There was no chance to be alone, no way to slip back and see if Surta had found his warning.

Sixteen

Buffalo Hunt

This cliff looks so much smaller from overhead, Y'keta thought. From down here, it seemed to cast a never-ending shadow on the flat granite ledge where the camp had been set up. Picking up a shard of the bleached white bone littering the bottom of the jump, Y'keta turned it over in his hands. This particular jump had been used by several tribes for at least 10 generations, and the bones at the base were piled far higher than a grown man's head.

Y'keta clambered up the narrow twisting trail to the top of the cliff, the loose shale and granite making each step risky. At the top, he could feel the hot wind blowing through his hair. If he closed his eyes, it was almost like flying. Almost.

As night fell, Y'keta was summoned to the Grey Lodge for a buffalo calling ceremony. Matra pulled a small green rock from her medicine pouch, and he watched, intrigued, as she spoke to the stone. "The People are in need," she told it, as though the rock was actually listening. "Summer is almost over and the winter will be harsh. Our elders need warm cloaks, and our children need your meat to stay strong." Bending over, she placed the stone in the middle of a scraped bull hide. The hide had been tanned so long ago it was basically white now, the intricate blue markings decorating it almost gone.

"Tiamat, we ask you to help the People," Matra pleaded. "Call to your brothers, the Buffalo. Give the great mother of the herd no wind of our presence. Teach our young warriors to run. Send them the scents of the wolf and the Kuniak to lead the herd into our reach."

Gesturing Y'keta forward, she had him sit in the centre of the massive white hide and placed a rolled-up buffalo calf skin in his arms. "This is the buffalo's child," she explained to the pulsing green stone. "He leads the great mother of the herd to our spears and arrows. Forgive him. He walks the only Road the People have. We are in need, and the buffalo spirit must come. Hear us."

The sound of the drums and the smell of sweet tobacco followed Y'keta into his dreams that night, and as he settled down to sleep among the warriors, his mind was filled with the thunder of hooves.

Before sunrise the next morning, Y'keta ran backwards and forwards along the buffalo run. He had to learn every bush, every rock; any hole might trip him when the buffalo were in chase. One mistake when he was running in front of the herd could mean his life.

The scouts had spotted the herd five days ago, and had been slowly coaxing them towards the top of the canyon since then. At night, the Scouts covered themselves with Kuniak skins and harried the tired animals, howling and baying at the herd, making sure none of the animals were actually resting or feeling secure.

It was a good-sized herd, D'vhan had said, over fifty animals and in good condition, fat from a summer of rich prairie grass and not too dried out by the scorching heat.

The elders and the oldest of the Green Feathers were gathering brush and stones to mark the path. Cairns of stones and piles of thorn bush marked every few feet, making an easy reference for Y'keta as he ran. And, at D'vhan's insistence, he was running it over and over and over.

§

On the third day, Y'keta stood at the top of the run, waiting for the herd to arrive. The dust in the air told him they were close. Soon they would crest the rise, and he would have to run for his life in front of a charging catastrophe.

Wrapping up in the Buffalo cloak and covering his head with the hood, he positioned himself where the herd would enter the draw. Waiting was hard, the buffalo hide was sweaty and the smell of tanning oil and leather was awful. I guess the mother won't be able to miss it, he thought.

Finally, after what seemed like half the morning was gone, Y'keta saw the cloud of dust rapidly approaching and felt the earth begin to shake under hundreds of pounding hooves. Quickly limbering up, he crouched down in a hollow at the side of the run. The first buffalo turned into the run, eyes red, chest heaving. Y'keta jumped up and ran into the middle of the lane, bawling so loudly his lungs burned with effort. The mother of the herd swung her shaggy head towards him. Flecks of spittle flew from her muzzle. As they rehearsed, the Kuniak behind the herd let out a full-voiced symphony of howls and barking noises. Frightened, the buffalo calf bawled loudly and started to run down the middle of the lane. The mother gave a bark. Her calf, Y'keta, didn't stop. Trying to catch up to what seemed, to her, to be a fear-stricken baby, she ran frantically behind him.

From behind each cairn and brush pile, the tribesmen jumped up as the main body of the herd entered the race. They started banging drums, shaking dry thorn bushes, waving hides;

anything to keep the herd panicked and on the move. The hunters behind the herd closed in as the great mass of sweaty fur stampeded down the lane and closer to the cliff.

Soon, Y'keta thought, very soon. The cliff edge was close now. He could see the white banner placed as a warning at the crumbling edge of the cliff. An opening appeared to his left. With his last strength, he ran between two elders waving hides, and dove for the pit they had prepared. Once he was in the hollow, the old warriors covered him with skunk weed and untanned hides, masking the smell of the buffalo calf from the mother buffalo, but almost choking Y'keta in the process.

He lay in the smothering darkness, wincing at the screaming and thrashing coming from the helpless animals as they went over the cliff. The force of the crazed animals running up from the rear was too much, even though the animals at the front had stopped, the rear of the herd ploughed into them, pushing them forward. One, two, five, ten at a time they poured over the edge of the cliff and landed screaming on the rocks so far below. Even in the pit and buried under the hides, Y'keta covered his ears. *I'm glad I'm not at the bottom of the cliff. I don't want to see this*, he thought. Once the sound died down, and the dust started to settle, one of the elders removed the covering from the pit that hid him, allowing Y'keta to climb out. He walked to the edge of the mesa and stared—he wasn't sure what it was he saw—it was blood, and pain, and the life of the tribe.

The warriors were standing like beads on a string along the edge of the precipice, firing into the brown gory mess at the bottom of the cliff.

The adults at the base of the cliff were wading through the thrashing madness, wielding daggers and spears to make sure the animals didn't suffer longer than necessary.

Gagging, Y'keta turned away from the cliff and walked towards the open plain. Whatever he expected the jump to be like, it wasn't this. The Waki'tani hunted. They caught game and fish, but they didn't ever take more than one meal at a time. There were always more fish, more nuts or berries, and the winter did not torment them as it did the people trapped on the ground.

Trudging down the steep path leading to the hunting camp, Y'keta saw a group of warriors standing around D'vhan. It took a while to reach them. His legs shook like leaves from the run. His mind felt foggy, elated at still being healthy, yet fighting with guilt at his role, no matter how necessary, in the hunt.

Noticing his distraction and the slightly lost look in his eyes, D'vhan put a warm hand on his shoulder. "Expect it, Y'keta, you were the buffalo child. Part of your Spirit fell with your herd. It is always so."

Pulling a small rock from his medicine pouch, he passed it to Y'keta. It was the Tiamat, the green rock Matra had used yesterday.

"Go," he said, shoving Y'keta towards the small creek meandering around the base of the cliff. "Clean up and take some time away from the camp. Talk to the Tiamat and let the buffalo Spirit leave your body."

Seventeen

Voices in the Storm

Dark clouds piled up over the lake. The peaks of the shadowed mountains looked like squat lodges against the horizon, their tops cut off by the grumbling black sky.

I am those clouds, Y'keta thought, trying to avoid the slow grey drizzle. He had spent the hours since leaving the hunting camp just sitting in the darkness under an overhanging pine tree. *Half cut off, lost and black.* Rubbing his sore feet and cramped legs, he watched the raindrops make patterns in the dark lake. *The best of me is gone. Like the mountains, I've lost my point.* A rustle in the nearby bushes gave him just enough warning to hastily bury the raven feathers he had been idly caressing under the mulch of leaves and twigs beside him. "I hear you," he said, trying not to sound as resentful as he felt.

"Only because I wanted you to," D'vhan replied. "You know it's the truth."

Y'keta smiled ruefully. "No one hears you unless you want them to," he said. "I think you are part night owl."

D'vhan made his eyes as big as saucers and hooted merrily. "Funny man," he said, "aren't you supposed to be more respectful to your elders, Kit'na?"

Y'keta just snorted. "If I clucked like a chicken every time you spoke to me, we'd all be eating eggs."

D'vhan settled down beside Y'keta, pulling his long legs up under his chin, trying to keep his feet out of the rain. "So, Buffalo Child," he said, "the whole village is around the campfire celebrating, and you, the hero of the hunt, are sitting here in the rain talking to thunderclouds."

"I needed the time," Y'keta said, hoping D'vhan would pick up on the hint and leave. "The run made me feel a bit shaky. I need to unwind."

"The run can do that," D'vhan said, "but I doubt it's the reason you are out here. I've seen you sitting outside of camp several nights, gazing at the lake, or watching the sky." Y'keta's stomach clenched as he realised hints were not going to be enough to make D'vhan leave him alone.

Y'keta shrugged, trying for a casual glance in D'vhan's direction. "I'm not used to so many people. The noise bothers me sometimes, especially since the caves."

"Everyone does it, you know." D'vhan's deep voice seemed part of the night, rumbling through the darkness like the thunder bouncing across the valley and over the lake. "I stare at fires. Pey't watches the inside of his wine cup. Laban sees things in the smoke of the smudge pots. The Greys call it soul voyaging. It's when one of the parts of your soul goes searching for the pieces it has lost."

With these words, the night became something more, as though the wind from the Sky Roads had blown across the conversation. Y'keta could hear each drop of rain, feel the dampness on his skin, even smell the mould-and-leaf stew the storm was churning up from the lake bottom. He shivered.

D'vhan's voice dropped lower, and he looked at Y'keta with frightening intensity. "You were the Buffalo Child today, Y'keta, the buffalo is now a part of your soul. You have to find a home for him among all the other voices your soul hears."

"Voices?" Y'keta asked, wrinkling his bushy brows at D'vhan.

Picking up a small rock from the ground at his side, D'vhan whipped it across the lake. *Plip, Plip, Plip,* it skipped three times before landing with a squelching noise.

"We are not only who we were born as, young one," he said. "Our parents gave us the first part of our soul at birth, but we add others to it as we grow and as the Sky Lords bring experiences to our Road. I was born in Atiskaat. Do you remember?" D'vhan inquired.

"I remember," Y'keta answered. D'vhan's unease around Siamaat, the mother of Atiskaat, was one of his strongest memories of that trip. It seemed so unlike the confident warrior leader.

"In Atiskaat, I was Dovhan, a child, just the youngest son of a household with too many sons. My mother had prayed to the Sky Lords for a daughter and got me." Reflectively, D'vhan touched the bright-red leathers he was wearing and the beaded necklace resting on his well-muscled chest. "I'm as close to a girl as she could have. I carry her voice and her woman-spirit in my head. As an adult, I left the village and became Kit'na here. I married, had children, and became D'vhan; another voice. Our children grew and left to find their own Roads, then my Iskine was lost to a lingering illness, and I became Widower, a third voice. I have run the buffalo both as Kuniak and as the Buffalo Child—those are also voices I bear. When we stare into the fire, or at the clouds in the sky, we invite those other voices to speak, to be heard and honoured. Think of it like asking friends to share a campfire. If there is a voice in your heart that you are afraid to invite, afraid to accept and to hear, that voice becomes like windstorm, howling forever in your ears. A lost child crying in the darkness, looking for warmth and home."

D'vhan rose slowly, content his message had been delivered.

"It took me many cycles to accept who I am and to embrace the new voices time brings to me." He said. "Much anger came from fighting the voices, and I hurt many people—good people—because of it. Don't wait."

Y'keta stared silently into the churning sky and let the thunder answer for him. It wasn't that he didn't hear D'vhan, but the voices were howling.

§

Y'keta woke up long before dawn. The overhanging branches had seemed so sheltering the night before, but now they were dripping cold rain down the back of his neck.

Limping back to camp, he slipped into the Red Lodge and stripped out of wet clothing. Nothing had ever felt as welcoming as pulling the warm sleeping furs over his shoulders and letting the soft warmth slowly draw all the cold from his bones.

D'vhan woke them all at dawn and sent them out to relieve the guards from Iniskin who had kept watch outside the village overnight. Tonight Sliat Village had the guard, tomorrow night it would be Esquialt. By then most of the hides would be dressed, and the drymeat made; the camp would break, and the villagers would start heading home.

The villages all made their own type of winter rations to trade. Esquialt made pemmican from drymeat, berries, and the melted fat from the kills all pounded together and preserved. With winter coming soon, the Mothers of each village would be busy organising trades to try to make sure the supply caches were full before they left for the trip home.

"Get moving," D'vhan growled at him, pushing his shoulders out of the doorway. "You're blocking the way, overgrown Hatchling." Y'keta had been in the Red Lodge too long for this to bother him. He stretched idly, taking his time, purposefully blocking D'vhan's path. Tomorrow they would be headed home.

Eighteen

Attack
<<<Siann>>>

The smell of smoke hung heavy in the calm night, and the quiet, hypnotic chirp of crickets drifted from the long grass. The hunt was over. We were on the way home, packs loaded with enough cured meat and hides for the winter as well as all the goods we traded for from the other villagers. As I fell asleep, I found myself obsessively rubbing the pink crystal I found a few weeks earlier, feeling it vibrate in my hand. Somehow the vibration seemed stronger, more urgent—almost a warning. It couldn't be real. Stones can't actually *mean* anything. Or so I thought until they came.

None of the guards gave warning. The first thing I heard was D'vhan screaming, "Red Lodge, up!" He swung wildly around with his daggers. The firelight was full of lumpy grey figures, about the right size, but somehow the wrong shape to be men.

I grunted as Y'keta landed on top of me with a harsh "Stay!" I was flat on my stomach, my head shoved down until my nose squelched in the mulch covering the ground. Laban was lying next to me, face dark as a thundercloud as Ren threw herself across his body, threatening to punch him if he didn't stay still.

I tried to turn my head to look for my mother, but Y'keta pushed me down again. "Don't move," he whispered. "We're out of the firelight. We need to stay unnoticed." Face first in the mud, all I could do was listen to the yelling and shuffling, feeling occasional bodies bump against my legs.

I heard Mother cry out and I tried to push Y'keta off me. I tried. Sun of Riad, I tried! "Let me go!" I yelled, not caring if the Utlaak were still there. "Let me go!" Kicking his shins and even trying to get my heel up between his legs didn't work. Desperately, I drove my head back into his face with a sickening crunch. Instantly, his hands on my arms loosened. I don't know where the strength came from, but I rolled him away from me. Shooting to my feet, I peered around the dark clearing. The Utlaak had kicked out the campfire, but I could still make out the familiar shapes of D'vhan and Pey't moving from shadow to shadow.

Fumbling forward, I tried to get across the clearing to where Matra had been sleeping. I tripped, looked down at the misshapen figure under my feet, and numbly stumbled across the clearing. My eyes swept from left to right across the lifeless bodies and the trampled grass until I saw her.

Stretching out from under a pile of the filthy grey corpses, her hand, with its crepe-paper skin and cracked fingernails, looked ghostly in the moonlight. I fell. Face down in the mud again. Mud and Blood and Maskim.

"Maskim!" I cried, my voice sounding like a child's echo of itself. Grabbing her hand, I pulled, trying to move her, trying to wake her. For the first time in my life, she didn't answer.

D'vhan grabbed me around my waist and lifted me into his arms, even as I kicked and screamed. "Shush, little one," he spoke slowly, as though to a wild animal, his large hand sliding over my mud-soaked hair in a soothing brush. "She Walks with the Elder Stars now; we cannot call her back."

It was cold. I watched the warriors move the dead Utlaak away from her and the Elders gather around to prepare her for the journey back to Esquialt. So cold.

Shivering in D'vhan's arms, I watched Sawiea bring in the bodies of the two guards who died before they had a chance to raise the alarm. She laid them beside Maskim. Suddenly remembering, I looked around for my brother. "Napaay?" I asked, terrified.

"He is well, little one," D'vhan murmured. "Iamaat has him with the other children. He did not need to see this."

So many fires were started that the campsite looked like a summer festival. Light to keep out the dark, I heard someone mutter. Or to reveal it, I thought, looking at the scaly grey hides of the corpses piled in the darkness at the side of the clearing.

Laban paced towards me across the too-bright clearing. He had something in his hands I couldn't—didn't want to—look at. "Siann." His voice, soft and low as the autumn breeze brought me no warmth. "Siann," he repeated, then with a bow, he placed Mother's travelling pack at my feet.

Everything she had felt necessary to carry with her day after day was in there. Grabbing the pack, I held it to my face and cried. It smelled like herbs, and strength, and Maskim; now gone.

§

The rest of the journey home was a blur. I woke, I cried; I walked, I cried; I sat—not sleeping— till I collapsed and slept.

I remember hearing my own voice screaming as the elders picked up Mother's carefully wrapped body along with those of the two murdered guards. It seemed so wrong to move them, but so wrong to leave them where they fell.

Hour after hour we walked without speaking. Larches became pines, prairie became rock as the mountain pass loomed ahead of us. I walked with the Elders, following the litter carrying what was left of Maskim. Taking her home, they said. How could we? How could it ever be home again? Home was on that litter.

For a while, Napaay walked with me, snuffling quietly. I hauled him, protesting, down the rocky trail. He didn't need to be carried. I needed to hold him, to smell the warm berries and baby smell of him.

It's not possible for a little one to stay quiet for long, and soon he was kicking to get down, darting back and forth between me and the children who walked with the Green Feathers further back.

"Go walk with Varas," I finally said, fighting a headache that felt like it would last for weeks. "Stay near to him though, Geeshoo, don't wander off." Just hearing him laugh at the silly nickname made my breath come a little easier. It pushed back the numbing fog that had surrounded me like a cloud since the attack.

Head pounding, eyes aching, I trudged down the ridge I had climbed only three weeks ago. No one played near the edges this time, no one wandered off to see what was over the hill. D'vhan had Red warriors at the front and rear of every section with strict instructions to keep the groups together.

The sky was a bright autumn blue; I hated it, it should be grey, it should be raining. D'vhan came up and walked next to me. "It will pass, Siann." His arm around my shoulder was supposed to be comforting. It wasn't.

No, I thought, *It won't.* D'vhan was almost a father to me. He had been my mother's best friend. Napaay was even named after his eldest son; how could he be here when she was gone.

Halfway down the pass we stopped to eat. The litter bearers switched out and went on ahead with their sad burdens. Sitting on the forest floor between Laban and D'vhan, I rolled the small pink crystal over and over in my palms. It was quiescent now, no vibrations, no warnings. No support there. No surprise.

Ren knelt before me, offering a bowl of warm broth.

"No."

"You must drink," she said. "Eating will come later, but you must drink."

"No."

Ren looked up at Laban and shrugged, an obvious *well I tried* gesture.

Laban looked at me. I'd always thought his pale eyes wise, now they just looked cold. He looked at the tired and frightened villagers and sighed. "If we need to, I will make you drink, Siann. The People need to get back to the Village, to a defensible shelter."

"Leave me *alone!*" I didn't think I yelled, but Ren looked shocked and turned away, her back stiff and offended.

I grabbed desperately at D'vhan's arm. "Make them understand," I pleaded, "I can't right now. I just can't."

Ren was rousing the weary villagers. They wanted to make it down to the bottom of the pass and into the forest's cover before we made camp for the night.

§

The trail wound against the gravel cliff like a drunken snake, but we made better time now the litters had gone ahead. The warriors who accompanied the dead would not stop until they reached the village and could guarantee our home was secure. I shuffled down the trail now with D'vhan beside me, then Laban or Ren. I think they were worried I might throw myself over the cliff edge. I felt like an unwieldy bundle of firewood the Elders had to haul down the mountain, slowing everything up and needing special handling.

We reached a corner two-thirds of the way into the lowlands, and something caught my eye. Far up above the trail, I could see a gnarled tree sticking out of a crack in the rock. I've no idea how it hung on up there, but its roots were dug in tight somewhere. On the top branch of the tree, there was something stuck. Either hanging or caught on the tallest branch, I thought. It might be a Raven's feather.

Staring up at the feather, wondering how it got here, so high up in the mountains, I didn't see Y'keta come up behind me until he almost bumped me off the trail. Without thinking, I put both my hands against his chest and shoved as hard as I could. The squat form didn't move an inch. Something in me broke. I needed to hurt him, needed to make him pay for what had happened to Maskim.

"Siann!" he howled as I punched and kicked him with all the pent-up force of this terrible day. Flailing wildly, I didn't even feel Laban's strong arms pull me away from Y'keta until I felt my blows hitting the air. "Let me go," I yelled from the bottom of my aching soul. "It's his fault. It's his fault!"

"If you must blame someone," D'vhan broke into my frenzy, his voice imperious and cold, "blame me. I ordered Y'keta to keep you out of the battle exactly the same way I ordered Ren to keep Laban out of the way."

An irritated male *humph* and a definitely female giggle came from behind me. I don't think Ren and Laban agreed on how she had followed those orders.

"You are the child of our Salixt. Laban is her second-in-command. Neither of you could be risked." Kicking a loose pebble over the edge of the cliff, I counted the moments until I heard it clatter to a stop far below. Maybe if I could push Y'keta hard enough.

"He should have left me," I raged, "between Ren and Y'keta they could have saved her!"

"No one could have saved her, child." Laban's voice was like smoke, soft and pervasive, colouring everything with a reasonableness I didn't want to acknowledge. "They targeted her, Siann. As soon as the attack started, the largest Utlaak charged towards the point where she was sleeping. All Ren and Y'keta would have been was two more corpses."

My head dropped onto my chest and I slumped, exhaustion sucking all the fight out of my body. I felt like someone had pulled the main pole out from under my tent. All the strength I had was collapsing into itself, leaving just billows of fear.

Nineteen

Grief and Freedom
<<<Siann>>>

Laban pulled me to the side of the trail, letting the others pass by. The dust kicked up by so many feet scurrying down the steep path coated my mouth and made me cough dryly. Slowly, the sound of feet faded and the thumping in my head let up a little as the usual rhythm of the forest re-established itself. "Just rest, little one," Laban said, wrapping his arms around me and sitting me on his knee, as though I were a baby.

His tunic felt rough on my cheek, the beads cutting in a little, but it felt so good to be held right now; to not have to deal with my life or anyone else's for just a moment. Laban crooned softly, almost too low for me to hear, but I found myself quieting just to listen to the nonsense words.

What seemed like a long time later, I was resting against his shoulder, watching the sun set orange over the mountains. "Talk to me,

Siann," he encouraged, "tell me what you are so afraid of."

"I don't know you." I waffled. I needed to talk, maybe needed even more to listen, past the raucous birds circling in my mind, squawking like a flock of Hania hovering over a corpse.

"You don't know me well," Laban said, "so I'm safe to talk to." Laban leaned back against a tree and stretched. "My heart is for Esquialt now, but you know I have been away since my youth."

Glancing sideways at Laban, I picked up a few dry pine needles and let them fall to the forest floor. I pointed out where one small cloud was scudding across the horizon, blown by a wind it couldn't see, going who-knew-where. "That's what I'm afraid of." I wrapped my arms tighter around myself and melted into the gathering shadows under the trees. "All my life I've been a cloud. Mother was the wind, always pushing me, always directing me. She decided what I did and where I went. Everything was planned to make me ready to be the next Salixt, to take up the cloak when she finally stepped down."

Laban's eyes shone at me in the darkness. It almost felt like he wasn't there—just eyes.

"I tried." My voice broke as I spoke. "I tried so hard to become all she was, to want what she wanted for me."

The darkening sky overhead was speckled with the first stars. Walkers on the Road, Matra would have called them, but now there was no Matra, no wind driving me, and I felt frightened, rootless, and free.

A rustle in the bushes had Laban reaching for the bone-handled knife slung around his waist. He held his hand up to silence me, and we sat frozen in the shadows, waiting. All I could think about was the grey forms of the dead Utlaaks piled around Maskim's body. I shook so hard it felt like my bones would rattle and give away our position.

We didn't sit there long, though. Ren came up the trail at a crouch and, with a wave, stepped under the boughs to join us. "It's too dark to walk down," she mumbled in her twangy voice. "I figured someone to stand guard would be useful." She shrugged and pulled out an oilskin-wrapped parcel from under her tunic. "Dinner." Ren started a small fire, and we passed around the mixture of drymeat and berries that had been made up at the hunting camp. The berries were still sweet, and the drymeat tasted so good when we washed it down with clean cold water from the skin Laban carried.

Putting Maskim's pack on the ground, I laid my head on it and watched Ren clean her knife and Laban sort the medicine stones in his pack. I must have slept for a while because the next time I looked up it was full dark. The Sky Road shone above us, from west to east, it crossed the sky, bright as the hope of forever. I could imagine Maskim walking that Road, catching up with Father and going on hand-in-hand as they had Walked in this life. The Dancers were out tonight as well. Green and blue carpets of flame hanging across the northern sky, and in the silence of the deep night I could hear the crackle and hiss of their dance.

Ren moved suddenly, surprising me. I thought both she and Laban were asleep.

"Not everyone Walks the straight road." She swept her arm from east to west, following the arch in the sky. "Some of us are like the Dancers, finding beauty and meaning in the dance, not only in the destination. We go here and there and do not find the Sky Road until later in our lives."

"Go to sleep, both of you," Laban's voice was groggy, "all this deep talk at such a late hour." Pulling Ren down beside him, he wrapped one of his furs over her and, with a wink at me, drifted off to sleep.

"I'm on guard," Ren muttered, getting a soft *grumph* from Laban in response. Then the forest got quiet, and nothing moved except the Dancers so far above. I watched them for a long time.

§

Morning came early, and we marched down the trail to catch up with the main party. Luckily, we could move a great deal faster than a party with elders and children could, and by mid-day we were all together again. I walked with Napaay for a while, listening to him chatter about a robin the others had seen that morning, and how much he had loved sleeping curled up in a pile with the dozen or so other children who were on the march. It wasn't far from the base of the mountain pass back to the winter village. I was put to work collecting firewood and starting the main campfire. For once, I didn't mind—anything to keep my thoughts from the four still bundles laid side-by-side at the edge of the clearing.

The lodges were all up by the time I got the campfire started. Even though the Elders had ordered a small lodge to be put up for Napaay and me near the main Grey Lodge, I knew it would be a long time before I felt like it was our home.

Twenty

At the Thunder Stones

Even though the pale sun peered down on the village, it felt like a grey morning. People were moving around the campsite slowly, getting back into a routine, finding things they had lost or packed, and generally tripping over each other trying to be normal. The Green Feathers settled around Iamaat's tent waiting for their tasks and lessons for the day. The Red Lodge was empty. Hunting parties were out and scouts were moving both inland and down the coast, looking for a sign of the Utlaak.

The Grey Lodge was empty. The ceremonial hide was in place over the door, but there was nothing but silence from within. Everyone from Siann, the youngest, to Hahnee, the fat cook, had disappeared just after dawn. Even Elder Inkiss, Laban's mother, had been carried out of the camp on a litter, complaining all the way because they wouldn't allow her to walk.

A few minutes north of the winter campsite was a sacred space in the forest, a clearing with a ceremonial ring in the centre, surrounded by four large boulders, burnt black by the Lightning. The grass inside the circle was stamped flat by generations of Grey feet. Siann, Laban, Hahnee, Inkiss, and the other Greys were sitting in the circle talking, the inconsequential chatter sounding more appropriate to a campfire than such a solemn occasion.

"Are we all here?" Inkiss' voice was soft and breathy as she leant against one of the boulders, shivering. She pulled her thick shawl tighter, but it was not enough to keep the cold of the stone from piercing her thin shoulders.

Hahnee took a quick look around the small group. "All are here, Eldest. We can begin."

"We have a thing to decide, children." Inkiss sounded like she was talking to the Green Feathers, and a ripple of laughter ran around the circle. "In our regular pattern, she who was Salixt would name a successor before she stepped onto the Road."

Here it comes, Siann thought, dreading the chains she felt wrapping around her. Inkiss' eyes caught hers. Though age had made them rheumy and colourless, they were still bright with intelligence and humour.

"But we are not in a typical pattern. The Utlaak have returned. While I honour Matra, both as our leader and as a shaman, she could not have known the burden would pass in such an uncertain time." Raising a stick-like arm to point at Siann, Inkiss intoned, "Siann dal Matra, in training and in heritage, you are the one who should become our next Salixt and leader of the Grey Lodge."

Siann's face paled as she breathed in sharply, her mind racing. *I can't do this. Don't make me do this!*

"But the world is not as it was before Atiskaat was attacked and Matra murdered," Inkiss said. "We face old enemies, and such a burden is hard to place on such young shoulders. We stand here between the Lightning Stones." Looking for a moment at her own weak legs, she rolled her eyes in frustration. "We *sit* here between the Lightning Stones, where the Elder Gods have always spoken to the Shaman of our people. And I ask you, Siann dal Matra, Grey child of Esquialt. What does your heart say? Will you Walk the Lightning Road and become our Salixt, or stand aside?"

Siann couldn't believe Inkiss was giving her a choice. For once in her life, her future would not be determined by her mother, her history, or the generations of Shaman before her. She could choose. "I loved my mother," she said, trying hard to remember what Ren had said about the Dancers. "And all my life I have honoured her wish that I train as shaman and eventually follow her as Salixt." Something inside her broke open. Finally, she saw a way out. "But it is not my Road." Siann looked around, waiting for lightning to strike, for someone to condemn her because she wanted more than a life chained to the village. "I will stand aside. Maybe in time, my Road will bring me to this decision again, but not now. For now, my heart has spoken clearly, and it says no."

"You honour your mother with your wisdom." Inkiss nodded, a smile flashing across her weathered face. "The goal every mother has for her children is for them to know themselves and walk their own Road. Since you have seen the Road before you so clearly, will you stand as Matra's voice in our midst and speak to the Tiamat for our People?"

"You wish me to speak for the Tiamat?" Siann's mind boggled at the thought.

"You are a shaman by birth and by training." Inkiss' voice was firm, though quiet. "I have no doubt some day you will hear the Lightning speak. It feels right asking you to do this."

She was right. Something in Siann's heart settled at the thought. The greatest gift she could give her mother would be to ensure her successor was chosen well, especially when war was likely. Carefully drawing the Tiamat from

Matra's travel pack, Siann held it up in front of the gathered Shaman. "I am youngest and least of my brethren." Siann looked at the faces surrounding her, each wizened, wise, and powerful. "Will you who are my elders heed the council of the Tiamat? Hear the Elder Stars speak in the voice of an untried child?"

Echoes of "We will," and, "Speak for the Stars, Siann," ran around the circle. Siann shook as she looked at the stone lying dead and flat in her hand. Matra had heard the Lightning, the Elder Stars knew her voice. How dare she think the stars would speak for her. Drawing her mother's knife from its sheath, she made a cut in the palm of her cupped hand and placed the Tiamat into the welling pool of blood.

"Green for our forest," she chanted softly, "Stone for the mountains we came from, Red for the blood that connects the hearts of the People. Sky Lords, breathe light into this, your creation. Speak the truth to your People. Find for us the heart of Esquialt." Matra's words seemed to echo in the clearing as Siann walked between the Thunderstones. "Elder Stars, hear your youngest daughter. Show our People the heart of Esquialt. Mark the one who is your Voice among the People."

Lightning forked down, a brilliant shock of white from the grey, overcast sky. Just above their heads, it split apart and hit each of the four

Thunder Stones, making them boom in protest. The power roared through them, then discharged into Siann from all four points of the compass, engulfing her in a blinding glare and making the Tiamat in her hand shine with the brilliance of an emerald sun.

"Laban of Esquialt," Siann spoke with the voice of the Thunder Stones, echoes of power in her normally soft tone. "The people of your Village have need, will you serve?"

Laban stepped forward jerkily, as though someone behind him had pushed him into the circle. Face pale and a little frightened, he looked at the child who stood at the centre of that voice. *What would this do to Siann?*

"Laban of Esquialt," the Thunderstones repeated. "The people of your Village have need, will you serve?"

"I will serve," Laban said shakily, "though I do not know why I am chosen over so many, who are so much more."

The roll of the thunder seemed to die down a little. "Heart of Esquialt, know this, you are chosen because you are needed, not because the others have any less power or worth. This time requires you. Hear us. Follow and serve." As the Thunder faded away, Siann was let loose from the grip of the Tiamat. She dropped like a puppet whose strings were cut, collapsing on the earth at the centre of the circle, clutching her left hand to her chest and rocking silently.

Hahnee ran forward, his fat face wobbling and worried. "Are you all right, Siann? What is wrong with your hand?" Carefully uncurling Siann's hand, he looked in astonishment at the perfect image of the Tiamat burnt into her palm. "We need a healer," he said, "someone bring herbs quickly!"

"I'm all right." Siann shook her head slowly. "It doesn't hurt at all." Wonderingly, she touched the round image on her palm and then lifted her hand to show the sign to the rest of the Shaman. A murmur ran through the circle at the sight. "What does it mean?" She said, "Has anyone heard of this before?"

"One thing I know," Laban said, recovering his balance quicker than the others, "no one will ever be able to ask you if you've heard the Lightning. You hold it in your hand!"

Twenty-One

The Road Before Them

The Grey Lodge walked back into Esquialt around midday. Laban walked at the front of the group with Siann just behind him. Movement around the village seemed to stop as the small group of shaman walked across to their lodge, and Laban removed the ceremonial barrier and led them in.

D'vhan and Y'keta just looked at one another and shrugged thoughtfully. "Someone's going to be surprised," D'vhan chortled, thinking of Ren out with the hunting party.

It was close to sunset when the Greys finally emerged from the Lodge, scattering to their own families and duties. Hahnee had been much missed, though apparently more as a cook than a shaman. A solemn quiet seemed to settle over the camp as the stars slowly appeared overhead. No campfire had been started, and the darkness in the camp echoed the deepening sky. Finally, when the Sky Road was clearly visible above,

D'vhan approached the Grey Lodge and began the ceremony to start Matra and the dead guards on their Road to the Elder Stars.

"Salixt, the Sky Road is calling. Who answers?" At the sound of D'vhan's voice, Laban walked out of the Grey Lodge for the first time as Salixt. He wore the beaded cloak, Red, Green, and Grey, representing all the People, and carried the Staff of Lightning and Thunder, for the Sky Lords and the Elder Stars. A quick mutter ran around the dark campsite, but it was silenced as the other Shaman stepped out from wherever they had been standing to form a loose semicircle behind Laban.

Moving through the village to the northern edge where the three bodies lay wrapped on their litters, Laban raised the staff over his head, intoning, "The Sky Road has called. Who answers?"

Hahnee stepped from the arc of Shaman behind Laban. His normally pudgy and placid face seemed transformed in the torchlight. "Salixt, Nia answers the call of the Road. She was a Warrior and strong for the People. Elder Stars, guide her home."

"Nia answers," the village echoed back from the darkness.

Savohn lit his torch and stepped forward. "Miskiwik answers." His light tenor voice caught on the words, "He was a child of our

Village. One of the Green Feathers I raised, and a Warrior of pure heart and mind. Elder Stars, guide him home."

"Miskiwik answers," chanted the echo.

If silence could get quieter, the village did then, knowing what would happen next. Siann lit her torch and stepped into the space beside Savohn and Hahnee. Napaay was standing beside her, clutching her hand tightly and sniffling back tears.

"Salixt, Matra answers." Siann's quiet voice filled the darkness, strangely potent and full of joy. "She led the People all her life with wisdom and with joy, she walks now to find my father and greet the Elder Stars."

"Nia, Miskiwik, Matra," Laban's voice was soft, barely heard between the torches and the stars. "We release you to the Elder Stars. Your journey goes on, as does ours. We will walk together again." Lifting the staff above his head, Laban reached far inside and touched the Lightning within. An eye-searing bolt shot down from the heavens, crackled through the staff and shot out to the empty forms which were once Villagers of Esquialt. Green and Blue fire danced over the wrappings for just a moment, and they were gone. A line of empty litters in front of the Grey Lodge was the only sign anything had happened. "The People have walked in darkness and loss." This time,

Laban's voice was loud and filled the clearing with the sound of his authority. "Let there be light now and an end to mourning." Once again, the Lightning flashed from Laban, this time a bright red and yellow flame ignited the central campfire and cast dancing shadows on the familiar faces surrounding it.

A large communal pot was put on the fire to warm, and soon Hahnee was ladling out a hearty stew to fill empty bellies and comfort chilled hearts. Quiet murmurs spread among the villagers as friends and family shared memories, and the rhythm of the nighttime camp reasserted itself.

§

The next morning, Laban ran around the campsite like a distracted ground hen, slipping and sliding on the skiff of snow that had fallen overnight, one eye on all the preparations and the other watching the trails for a sign of Ren's return. The hunting party returned just before mid-day, their bags bulged and thumped at their thighs, and several of the warriors had kaal or other large animals slung over their shoulders. They strode into camp together and headed across the busy clearing to deliver their kills to Hahnee for salting and processing. A lightning-fast smile flashed through Ren's eyes as she saw Laban working his way across the clearing to her side.

"Greetings, Little Hawk." His pale grey eyes warmed at the sight of her. "You had good luck on the hunt, it seems." Such formal words, cool and even a bit distant, but there was nothing cold about the fire in his eyes or in the gentle warmth of his hand on her cheek. Laban turned to Hahnee while Ren emptied her pouches. "Do we have enough food built up," he asked. "I am not sure how Matra typically arranged winter supplies."

Hahnee's face broke into a brilliant smile. "I will make it enough, Salixt."

Ren blinked. "Salixt?" She looked at Laban again.

Hahnee winked at her merrily. "You missed a few things while you were gone." Chuckling, he picked up the meat Ren had brought in and waved them away. "I have work to do before night meal."

Laban led her towards the Grey Lodge, taking her hand and making her look at all the villagers suspiciously. No one was paying attention. They all deliberately looked the other way with strange little smiles on their faces. Nothing made Ren more nervous than thinking someone knew something she didn't—and thinking everyone knew something was driving her crazy. Even Laban had a smirk hiding in the corners of his mouth as he gently gripped her elbow and steered her into the Grey Lodge.

"I'm not supposed to be in here," she said, "what do you think you're doing?"

Laban didn't answer, he simply pulled her head down to his kiss and made her forget why she was talking. Without thinking, she wrapped her arms around his waist and leant into his chest. Her arms crept up to hold on to his broad shoulders as the ground beneath her disappeared.

"Laban," she said. "What are we doing in here? It's wrong."

Laban's hand drifted down her back to rest at her trim waist and pull her closer to him with a softly sighed "Mmm."

Her body seemed to fit his, despite the height difference, and wherever their bodies touched she melted. "We'll get in trouble."

"Shush, Little Hawk, I am allowed to be in my own lodge."

Kissing her seemed far more important to Laban than explaining. He tugged gently on the long wheaten braid wrapped around his hand and when Ren brought her head up, eyes glassy and unfocused, he took advantage of the movement to slide his warm lips down the arc of her throat to nibble at her collarbone. Ren knew there was something important she needed to talk to Laban about, but her mind seemed full of fireflies, each one setting fire to her body in new, unexplored ways. Her hands moved around to Laban's chest, riding up the hard muscles. Ren jumped back as her palms slid over his nipples, and he let out a growl. "What are we doing?" She felt Laban's heart racing under her palm. "It's crazy." Her voice was so soft that she didn't even recognise the sound.

"Quiet, my love." Reaching behind her, Laban pulled at the tie holding the door flap open. As it swished into place, enclosing them in the dimness of the lodge, she felt a jolt of panic run through her.

She didn't know how to do this, how to be loving, how to be in a relationship with someone.

"I want to show you something," Laban spoke softly and slowly, as though he was gentling a wild animal. Taking her hand, he led her into the private area of the lodge, behind the cedar screens, where the Salixt lived. The smell of the cedar, warmed by the pale autumn sunshine, surrounded them as Laban wrapped his arms around her from behind and turned her around in the centre of the room. It took a moment for her to see what he was trying to show her. All their things were in this room, from his bedroll, her bundle of dried Vair berries, everything from his old lodge. "This is my home now. I have been chosen as Salixt of the People. I wish this to be your home also. I cannot ask, Ren. I can only hope that staying with me, tying yourself to the Road and to the People I am called to serve, is something your heart can accept." His voice was so quiet. He sounded humble, as though he hadn't just asked her to accept him, the Elder Shaman of Esquialt, Salixt of the Village, as her mate. She brought nothing, no family, no people, nothing, but he was waiting humbly for her choice, for her to answer him. "This is too sudden." His voice was rough, as though tears were creeping into it. She had taken too long to answer.

"All my life I have belonged to no one, had a place nowhere," Ren mumbled, looking down, voice almost inaudible. This was the truth at the heart of who she was, and her throat closed as she forced the harsh words into the quiet of the lodge. "My parents died before I was old enough to walk. I was raised grudgingly, by the Eldest Mother. No one wanted a child whose family was touched by such misfortune. I grew up knowing I would leave as soon as I was able. Knowing they would feel relief when I left." Ren shook her head at the absurdity and murmured, "You, who hold not only the heart of the People, but my heart, ask me to stay. You want me to tie my Road with yours and let us walk together until we join the Elder Stars?"

"I don't ask, Ren," Laban repeated, a faint hope flickering in his pale eyes. "I have nothing to offer you. My life will be full of difficult decisions and there will never be an end to this responsibility. I will not leave this village or these people again until I am released to walk the Sky Road. But, Little Hawk, I will give to you all I have, or will ever have in this world, if you will walk it with me."

"Oh Laban," she said, "you offer me all I could ask for in this world." Her long-fingered hands cradled his face as she turned it up so she could place a gentle kiss on his firm lips. "I don't need to be the mate of a Salixt or a shaman, but my Path would go down into darkness and my heart would freeze forever if I had to walk apart from you."

"The Stars shine in your eyes, my love," he responded with the formal words of Atiskaat's marriage proposal. "Will you join your Road with mine and journey to the Elder Stars with me?"

Her green eyes misted with tears as Ren gave back the ritual answer. "Our Roads have always been joined, my love. We had but to find each other to walk them."

A raucous noise from outside the lodge interrupted Ren's tears and Laban's quiet joy. With a last gentle stroke of his hand down her cheek, Laban rose and led her out of the Grey Lodge. The evening campfire had been lit, and he stood within its light to pronounce a blessing on the night and the meal. "Are we well,

Esquialt?" he asked as the people gathered around the central fire drawn by the drums and the smell of Hahnee's kaal stew.

"We are well," the villagers answered, relaxed and reassured by full bellies and the comfort of the ritual ending to their day.

"May the Elder Stars shine on your path and may the Sky Road always stand before you." The traditional night blessing of the shaman echoed across the clearing. "May the night bring you peace and the day be filled with purpose and joy." They waited for Laban to step back and complete the ritual, but he didn't. "I am also well," he said. A few eyebrows rose. This was different, a change to the unchanging ceremony. "Ren Ut'yaat, Red daughter of Esquialt, has agreed to join her Road to mine and become my mate." Laughter and congratulations swept through the camp. Above them, the Elder Stars danced with joy.

Ren tried to escape into the shadows but was dragged back by D'vhan, who fussed and clucked over her like he had arranged the marriage himself. "I knew it," he husked. "I knew he was waiting for you to come home from the hunt!"

Later, in the quiet of the Grey Lodge, they discussed families and ceremonies and all the necessary details for tying their Roads together. The talk went late and didn't stop until Laban blew out the oil lamp and softly growled, "Enough, Little Hawk." He folded her in his arms and in the silence of the night.

WINTER

Twenty-Two

Snowbound
<<<Siann>>>

Spring had to come soon. The People were
starving. Shivering, I pulled the thick furs
tighter around my shoulders as I watched the
hunters drift away from the sleeping camp. The
fact that the camp was quiet so long after
sunrise was another sign that the winter had
been hard, far harder than usual. Worrying at
my bottom lip didn't help, it was already sore
and chapped. Supplies must be running
dangerously low. D'vhan was only sending four
hunters today. Each would need trail food for
three days, along with whatever they could find
in the bush. Sending out four warriors, instead
of the usual six, meant that twelve days of
drymeat and berries went with them, not
eighteen.

Some of the elders had not left their lodges
in days, not even to come to the campfires. "The
People need warmth, not only the warmth of

their lodges but of each other's company," Laban insisted when an elder questioned him about the wisdom of burning much-needed fuel on the nightly ceremony. "They need to know that they do not walk alone in the dark." Several of the oldest had Walked this winter, taking the Sky Road to the Elder Stars.

I watched Y'keta try to coax a spark from wood made sullen by last night's snow. *If he can't make a fire,* I thought, *it couldn't be done!* Y'keta had lightning in his blood. If he looked at a fire or walked close to one, the blaze would jump and seem to roar towards him. But today even he was struggling. The wood was sodden and dry tinder scarce. Finally, I saw a hint of smoke and watched as he carefully nursed the central campfire to life.

I guessed we were all cooking together again, bringing everything we caught or gathered, putting all the remaining food in one pot. It was one way to make sure no one had extra while the weakest went hungry. Grabbing Napaay by his hand—not pudgy anymore—I pulled him away from the fire and into the bush surrounding the winter camp. The camp was in a quiet valley, usually home to a large herd of kaal and a lake that never froze. This year wasn't typical though. The kaal didn't migrate south. They stayed on the plain and died, crippled by the deep snow, and helpless before the starving packs of kuniak.

"Let's dig up some roots for tea," I tried to encourage Napaay, forcing myself to sound happy with the prospect of bitterroot tea, again. "We want to bring something to put in the pot for supper tonight."

"I don't want tea," Napaay whined. "I'm hungry. I want grain, and berries, and…"

Pulling him into my arms, I tried to comfort both of us with a big hug. "I know you are hungry, little goose. We all are, but spring will come soon and the kaal will be back, and we will feast until we burst."

"I won't burst." Napaay nodded firmly. "But Uncle Pey't will. He's too big to eat one more bite of kaal." That was true in the summer, but even Uncle Pey't was gaunt now. Lung fever had burned through the warriors' Lodge, weakening many of them and causing a constant cough that made sleeping difficult, if not impossible. As the oldest of the warriors, it had hit Pey't and D'vhan the hardest. Pey't had not been out to the campfire in a few days.

§

The snow piled up outside the lodge, white mountains of beautiful, pristine death. Y'keta trudged between the lodges, coughing and cursing at his cold, wet feet.

"Get in the lodge," D'vhan said.

"You first, old crow," Y'keta taunted. "If an old bird like you can stand the watch, I can!" Y'keta peered at him. The winter hadn't treated D'vhan well. His normally wiry frame looked as though the skin was stretched over too much bone, the deep voice reduced to a gravelly whisper. "I can keep my eyes open. Get inside, D'vhan." Bossily, he waved the Elder into the lodge and took up his watch post near the smudgy remains of the fire. Grabbing a few twigs and some dried bark from under the edge of the lodge, Y'keta carefully fed the fire, blowing on it gently to encourage the ashes to catch. There wasn't much wood left, and he could keep the fire going with less firewood than anyone else would need.

Shivering, he pulled the hide across his shoulders and tried to listen to the howling voices in the wind. As always, he heard the Buffalo Child crying and D'vhan lecturing him on accepting the different parts of himself. *Easy for D'vhan to say*, he thought. D'vhan had pieces of the People, pieces of the forest, the widow, the Red Lodge, natural pieces of a natural world. *How am I supposed to make the pieces fit for me? My pieces are so broken. Pieces of the People, the forest, the sky, all mixed up with the memories of being captive in the Utlaak burrows.* The memory of the absolute darkness in the tunnels still panicked

Y'keta, making it difficult to sleep in the lodge
some nights. He had to be near a door or a
smoke hole, needed to be able to see the stars
and convince himself he wasn't still in the
burrow.

I broke, he thought. *I know I did, even if no
one else saw me.* His eyes burned as he
remembered the hours spent imagining his sister
Netta held captive in the dark, broken and
dying. She had died alone down there, because
of him. He had cried like a child, like a man, for
the first time accepting there was nothing he
could do to fix the mistake he had made.
Nothing he could say, nothing he could give that
would bring her back. His father had told him
exploring the burrows was dangerous, but he
had to go. He had to see what was under the
green ocean of trees at the bottom of his world.
Well, he had dropped through the bottom, and
he was still falling, this time with no-one
hovering above him to pull him out if he went
too far.

A soft touch on his shoulder made him
jump. He hadn't realised he was whimpering as
he nursed the flickering flame. "Rest," D'vhan
told him. "It is hard enough to keep the fires
going in the campfire without burning yourself
with fever and with recrimination." Handing
Y'keta a small hollowed-out gourd, he gave him
a gentle push towards the Red Lodge. "Drink

and sleep," he rasped. "The living can learn, the dead cannot. Spring will come, and with it will come the peace the winter winds seem to steal. I have seen enough winters to know everyone feels the cold wind in their soul now and again."

Shifting miserably, Y'keta downed the sleeping potion, grimaced, and walked towards the Lodge. "Thank you, old crow," he murmured, not sure if D'vhan heard, "for everything."

§

The next morning the drifts had extinguished the campfire and D'vhan was gone. No body, no blood, no footprints walking onto the Road, just gone. Y'keta cursed, swore, and rampaged around the camp. *How could he do this to me? To let me sleep, knowing he was planning on walking away. D'vhan wouldn't go without warning us unless he had a reason.* Y'keta fumed. *He left to make the supplies for the villagers last until spring.* They would find him fairly close, eyes closed and a crooked, superior grin on his face, the one he wore when he thought he'd gotten away with something.

Pey't and Sawiea didn't speak, but grabbed their weapons and stuffed medicines and blankets into their packs. They looked at Laban, obviously not asking permission, and set out into the frozen brush. "The lake," Sawiea pointed out. "He'll go to the lake." Their snowshoes made good time on the frozen trails. They didn't call out. D'vhan wouldn't answer— stupid, noble old crow. They forged ahead silently until they reached the lake shore. The ice on the lake was thick and covered with snow.

"He hasn't made it yet." Sawiea sobbed in relief. "No breaks in the ice. We've still got time."

Quickly making a fire and building a snow wall between it and the forest, the two hunters settled to wait. "What are you doing?" Y'keta's voice crackled with impotent rage. "He could be anywhere out there dying."

"Quiet, Hatchling," Pey't said, "be silent and learn."

Things quieted for a while and pretty soon the fire and the warmth of the snow shelter made Y'keta warm and sleepy. His head was nodding, eyes closed when the end of Sawiea's bow tapped him lightly, making him jump.

"He's coming," she mouthed, her voice barely audible. "Get ready for a quick run. We have to catch him before he hits the water."

Sawiea and Pey't squatted behind the snow wall they had made. Even breathing too hard might alert the wily old crow and lose them the chance to save him.

I will catch D'vhan, Y'keta reassured himself. *Even if I have to call on that other self*

*and put on my wings to do so. The Red leader
will not die.* It had been almost a year since he
had tried to use that other self. Would his
muscles still know how?

The crackle and crunch of footsteps were
getting closer. "He's ill," Pey't said, "or we
wouldn't even hear him!"

Y'keta nodded. D'vhan was part owl, they
all thought so. No one heard him unless he
wanted to be heard. Y'keta remembered a
summer night in the rain. Hearing D'vhan
approach and mocking him for the noise he
made. Something was wrong. He felt it. "What
did you say?" he asked Pey't a bit sharply.

Pey't gave him a pointed look and shushed
him. "What I told you, noisy, you would never
hear D'vhan unless he wished to be heard."

"Exactly!" Y'keta stood, hearing the
laughter in the bitter wind, and peered over the
snow wall. "Okay, old crow," he bellowed at the
falling snow. "You've had your fun. Now stop
it!" D'vhan wasn't there. Footprints moved up
to the base of their snow wall and disappeared
north into the storm.

"D'vhan, no!" Sawiea yelled in anguish. She
left with Pey't, headed north, following the line
of deep imprints. Y'keta took a step or two after
them and stopped suddenly. Something was
wrong with this. D'vhan was much too canny. If
he had set up this charade so carefully, he

wouldn't leave great big boot heels showing where he'd gone. Walking around the base of their snow wall, Y'keta found a soft mound of freshly disturbed snow. Poking at it with his foot, he dug out D'vhan's old snow boots.

Nice work, old man, he thought. *You walked backwards to the wall, buried the boots, and light-footed away...but which way?*

For the first time in months, he wished he could take to the air. *I may not have the wings,* he thought, *but I can find the old man even in this storm.* Pushing back the hide he had wrapped around his head, Y'keta tuned out the wind, turned down the cold, and focused on the one sound he needed to hear. Faint, and far away it was—crunch, crunch, slip, crunch, bare feet crashing through the crust of snow. Drawing on the training he'd received from D'vhan and adding the skills he learned as a hatchling from Surta, Y'keta stepped into the storm. Surta had always told him to trust sound and smell over sight when the weather was poor.

Emptying his mind of the winter and the wind, Y'keta reached for the faint scent that followed D'vhan. The mixture of tainflower and tallow he used to seal his skin against the wind and weather. D'vhan had used it for so long now that the rich, warm scent permeated everything he owned. It was as much part of him as the

black leathers and the coarse red hair. After a
few frantic minutes, he caught the scent. It
seemed to be coming from the inlet south of
them. Stepping lightly, trying to spread his
weight across as much snow as possible, Y'keta
stalked his prey.

Oh no, old man, he thought. *You are not
making my life worse by being noble. You will
starve along with the rest of us.*

The dead pine needles underfoot made
progress either noisy or painfully slow. Y'keta
chose slow. D'vhan would bolt for the ice if he
heard a sound behind him. Without a surprise
advantage, Y'keta knew, he couldn't hold the
older warrior by force. The swirling snow ahead
seemed to clear for a moment and allow a
glimpse of a grey shuffling body approaching
the water. *Now,* Y'keta thought as loudly as he
could, *you've tricked us, we've gone north, stop
to prepare. You have time for prayer, time to sit
and accept this ending, time to say goodbye.*

As though Y'keta had willed it to happen,
the figure dropped to its knees in the snow,
making gestures Y'keta recognised as part of the
death rituals of the village. Ten more paces,
five, finally Y'keta sprang from the pine brush
and landed on top of the shivering old man. "Oh
no you don't, old crow," he said, wrapping his
arms around the struggling elder and pinning
him face-first in the snow.

"Leave me." D'vhan said, "I am your elder. You will obey!"

Y'keta's squattish brow furrowed. "You are as dear to me as my father, and I will not allow you to destroy yourself. You are needed here."

"I can give nothing to the Village now," D'vhan explained. "I am too worn to hunt, too sick to work. I take food and shelter the others need. Now leave me."

Y'keta stared at the wrinkled brown face. "Listen to me, D'vhan. You must survive this winter. If you cannot survive it, what hope do the other elders have? They will walk away thinking they help the Village, as you have done. Our wisdom, our history, all will be gone when this killing winter ends! You cannot set this example. You have been the strength of the Village for all your days. You cannot show them weakness now."

Taking his cloak off and wrapping D'vhan in its warmth, Y'keta picked up the frail elder and carried him back towards the village. As soon as he entered the Red Lodge carrying the fragile bundle, he was surrounded by anxious villagers demanding to know if D'vhan was all right.

"Shh," Y'keta said. The old warrior in his arms, stirred, but didn't open his eyes. "Don't wake him. He's enough of a handful when he's sleeping!"

"Too late," D'vhan's voice was a faint echo of its regular bass rumble. "So now you've dragged me back in," he said, "what are you going to do with me?"

"Not me, I'm not punishment enough." Y'keta smiled sweetly. "I'm turning you over to Sawiea until you're better." He watched as D'vhan squirmed at the thought of Sawiea fussing over him.

"Not her," he cranked. "She'll chain me to a bed and make me into a baby."

"It serves you right." Y'keta was unmoved. "Time for you to learn that taking care of us means looking after yourself."

Against his protests, D'vhan's bedroll was dragged close to the fire, and he was unceremoniously handed into the care of Sawiea. She approached his pallet tentatively. "So, old crow, you haven't managed to kill yourself yet." Sawiea's voice was quiet, although her eyes flashed ferociously. "If ever you try running off again, I will tie you to the lodge pole!"

Taking a bowl of heated water from one of the hovering Red Feathers, she gently washed his coarse red hair and, using a comb of carved bone, brought some kind of order to the unruly mop.

"You are not alone," she murmured so that none of the others would have a chance of hearing. "I know Iskine is gone, and you think you have nothing to tie yourself to the Village, but you are wrong! You have a purpose here! You are not alone!"

"I'll be out of bed and back to normal in a few days if not less." D'vhan said, "I don't need all this fussing over."

"Well I need to fuss, so be quiet, old crow," Sawiea ordered, her gentle hands belying her stern tone. "It's my turn to be in command."

§

But D'vhan didn't come out of the Lodge in a day, or a week, or a whole moon cycle. Sawiea sat by his side as he shook with fever, his breathing laboured and hoarse. By the time she allowed him to sit up and answer Laban's many questions about the day-to-day running of the Village, spring was coming.

Twenty-Three

Questions Without Answers

Finally, the howling winds subsided and the ice in the middle of the lake began to crack and melt. Something in the softness of the air had everyone looking for the spring. Even the frailest of the elders ventured out now and again to look at the pale-blue sky and take deep breaths of the cold, fresh air.

D'vhan was still whispering, his voice wispy and quiet. Sawiea and the Red Feathers clucked around him like hens with only one chick, fetching and carrying for him until he wheezed that he should have caught lung fever cycles ago. Right now, he was sitting on a thick pile of furs outside Red Lodge, head resting on his chest, supervising through closed eyelids as some of the young Greens mended and cleaned armour for the Lodge.

"D'vhan?" One of the little ones tapped his knee to get his attention.

"Humph!" he exclaimed as his eyes shot open and his head straightened. "Yes, Hatchling, what is it?"

The surprised hatchling jumped back, wary of the wide-awake warrior leader. "Iamaat told me you killed an Utlaak at the battle? The one where Matra..." The high, peeping voice broke off.

"I killed several of them." D'vhan's face scrunched into a dark scowl.

The youngling rushed on, and all in one breath blurted, "Is it true they are animals that can't think or talk?"

"Well, now." D'vhan looked around for a convenient escape route from the hatchling's curiosity. "Oh, there is Y'keta, he survived three moons in the burrows of the Utlaak. He's the one you should be asking."

Suddenly, a dozen pairs of eyes fixed on Y'keta, who was walking back from the lake, catch in hand. The wily old crow waved once at the unsuspecting warrior and slipped inside the entrance of the lodge. From knee-high to hip-high, the Green Feathers jumped around Y'keta like a school of fish after a rainstorm.

"Y'keta, teach us about the Utlaak," they said. "What do they look like? Where do they come from? Can they think and talk like us? Please tell us, please, Y'keta!"

"Peace, Hatchlings." He laughed merrily all the while planning instant and painful vengeance on the elder warrior. "Let me give this fish to Hahnee and I will answer some of your questions." He walked the brace of spotted reed-fish over to Hahnee's tent, hoping the delay would help him lose the tail of children who had followed him since he reached camp. It didn't work.

As soon as he handed the fish over and left Hahnee to plan supper for the village, the piping clamour started again, "Please, 'Keta!"

Laban watched Y'keta walk around the village, children chasing after him, like a young comet with a tail of green fire. "You may as well tell them," he said. "They'll learn something, perhaps, and they'll leave you alone."

Y'keta doubted it. Answers had never satisfied his curiosity, all they had done was create new questions. Shrugging, he flopped down on the stack of hides D'vhan had abandoned and smiled at the eager faces. "Three questions. That is all I have time to answer right now. Make them good ones."

A quick huddle among the children brought consensus, and one of the older ones, a young man of ten or eleven, asked the first question. "Where do the Utlaak come from?"

"Well, that is a bit of a tricky question." Y'keta's broad brow wrinkled as he tried to find an answer satisfying for the children without giving them too many specifics. "They come from the world, the way we all do, placed here when the Sky Lords set the Road in motion." At the outcry from his audience, Y'keta laughed. "But I don't think that's the question you are asking. You want to know where the Utlaak live. They live below ground, but not in the tunnels. There are caverns in the mountains that we have never seen. Their villages and homes are there."

The chattering rose again as the children decided on their next question. Apparently this decision was a bit more difficult given the number of *you-saids* required before a choice was made. Finally, they asked, "What did you see when you were in the tunnels?"

Y'keta's face paled. A lot of what he saw in those tunnels was not for young ears. He still wasn't sure about some of it. His mind had been so fractured at the time. "Dark, lots of dark," he murmured. The frowns and muttering warned him he wouldn't get away with such a simple answer. "Honestly, young ones, I was chained in one room, so all I saw were the piles of weapons and food moved in and out of the tunnel where they kept me, and the Utlaak themselves—two kinds, the big ones and the little ones. I don't know their proper names."

"Last question, and make it a good one," D'vhan wisped at the children from where he was leaning against the post of the Lodge. "Y'keta is in my spot, and I need my rest!"

After several squabbles and one *I'm going back to the lodge* fit, finally, one of the eldest children stepped out and decided herself what the last question would be. "We have lots of questions, Y'keta, but my last one would be this. What did you learn from being in the tunnels, and will it help us fight the Utlaak now?"

Scratching his short hair, Y'keta wondered if a new shaman had spoken. "Some of what I learned will help us be ready for the Utlaak if they attack. They fear fire. The big ones are nasty, the little ones only attack because they're scared of the big ones."

"Now, back to your tasks, Hatchlings," D'vhan rasped. "I'm sure Iamaat will be expecting to see you before the midday meal." He didn't need to raise his voice. The mention of the Green Leader had the children scampering to finish whatever task she had assigned for the morning.

"Thank you." Y'keta stood up and offered the sunny spot to the old warrior. "But don't think I've forgotten who got me into this!"

D'vhan chuckled evilly—or, at least, tried to until the laughter turned into a strangled coughing fit ending up with him crashing down on the sun-warmed hides with a thump.

"Salixt of Esquialt," a stranger's voice overpowered the sound of D'vhan's coughing.

"I am Laban of Esquialt," Laban answered, stepping out of the Grey Lodge hand in hand with Ren. "Who hails me?"

Outside stood a tall, broad-shouldered warrior of middle age and excessive girth. His spear bent as he leant on it puffing breathlessly. D'vhan and Y'keta drifted closer, putting the newcomer between them. Ren instinctively drifted left, making a defensive pyramid covering the visitor from every side.

"I am Tiat of Iniskin. I bring word that my Salixt, Emial, will arrive within three days for the festival. She ordered me to come ahead and aid with preparations."

"My thanks, Tiat." Laban bowed politely, throwing a quick sideways glance at D'vhan. "D'vhan, will you take Tiat into Red Lodge for the night. Tomorrow we will finish the lodges for the visiting Shaman and their people."

D'vhan caught a swift movement as Laban's face twitched, lips pointed towards the Red Lodge. "Of course, Salixt. Tiat is welcome, as will be any Red Lodge brother who comes to the festival. Let me show you where you can sleep." *And where I can find out a bit more about you,* D'vhan thought as he led Tiat towards the Lodge.

Before night meal, three more warriors had entered camp, all representatives of Shaman who would be arriving in the next few days. Even Amakil, the only surviving warrior from the ruin of Atiskaat, had come. He brought the news that Savohn would be arriving with the morning tide.

Twenty-Four

A Risky Request

Y'keta watched as the shaman of the four closest villages arrived, each with their small retinue of warriors. The festival would begin tomorrow. For three days there would be ceremonies and feasts. The tribes would hunt together and the Mothers would bargain and trade, trying to replace the supplies the winter had swallowed.

Why, Y'keta thought, *do I feel like my crest, if I still had one, would be standing straight up. Something just isn't right.* He had tried to talk to D'vhan, but he was busy playing host to the dozen warriors who had come from other villages. He passed Y'keta's suspicions off as the natural paranoia of a warrior when there were strangers in camp. D'vhan saw nothing out of the ordinary. This was what happened every year.

Walking around the perimeter of the camp, Y'keta noticed the rapidly melting snow and the muddy paths leading into the Village, now churned up by the extra bodies here for the festival. He saw Siann sitting outside the small lodge they had built for her when they had returned from the hunting camp. *In her own way, she's been banished, too,* he thought sadly. She's even lost Napaay now that he is living with the other hatchlings in the Green Lodge. It felt odd to have any reason to sympathise with Siann. She looked too peaceful. Y'keta had to disturb her. "Siann, can I talk to you for a moment?"

Siann jerked, spoiling the hide she'd been copying. "Shards, 'Keta! I worked on this hide all morning and you've spoiled it!" Her face filled with thunderclouds, and her lightning-touched brown eyes glowered. "I should fry your hide!"

"I am sorry, Siann. I didn't mean to startle you." Y'keta sounded repentant, but his odd golden eyes bubbled with laughter. "I do need to talk to you though, it's important."

Gesturing to the fallen log beside her, Siann carefully scraped the ink from the spoiled hide and rolled it tightly to put it away. "What's wrong?" Siann waited for the usual barb or insult, but it didn't come.

"Can I ask you something unusual?" Y'keta cast quick looks around at the clearing and spoke in a rush. "Have you pulled out the crystal you found on the way to the high prairie lately? You told me it vibrated like it was trying to warn you when Matra...when the last attack happened."

Siann hadn't. Fishing through her pack, she pulled out the piece of crystal and rubbed it between her hands. The stone flamed in her palm, and Siann dropped it on the floor. Picking it up carefully, Y'keta watched as the fire died in its heart and it turned back into a simple pink rock.

"How did you make it do that?" He peered at the dead lump in his hand.

"I rubbed it in my hands." Siann shrugged. "It's never shone before, I've no idea." Siann gingerly took the stone back from Y'keta's hand. It flared as she touched it. A burning red sun flashed in the heart of the stone and died down to a warm glow as the stone settled into her hand. "Laban—we need to find Laban. This shouldn't be happening." Siann got up to find the Elder Shaman, but Y'keta stopped her, grabbing her arm, and not gently.

"Please," he insisted, "try to see if the stone is warning you. Maybe I'm paranoid, but something is prickling at the back of my neck and ruffling my feathers."

Siann looked warily at the stone, closed her eyes, and cupped it in both hands. "If it's vibrating now, it's not much," she said. "There is something there, but not close, not today. If you are this worried, and the stone is active somehow, Laban needs to know, and quickly."

Y'keta was thinking as fast as he could—warnings, snow, that odd stone, it all added up to something, and it wasn't good news. "You go to the Salixt and ask about your stone. I'll talk to D'vhan about the guards and security, and I'll be there in a few minutes."

Siann nodded and headed out to find the shaman. It took longer than she thought. Finally, she found Laban, D'vhan, and Hahnee huddled around one of the outer campfires, planning meals for the visiting Shaman, the last of whom were to arrive in the morning.

"Excuse me." She smiled apologetically at Hahnee. "May I talk to you for a moment, Laban? You too, D'vhan."

Hahnee nodded at Siann and went back to cutting vegetables for the night meal. Taking a nose-twitching sniff of the spice bundles for tonight's stew, he sighed in anticipation. He knew his job—he didn't need nervous Elders telling him how to prepare meals.

"What is it, Siann?" Laban's voice was respectful, as always, but it had been even more so since the night the Lightning had spoken through her and made him Salixt.

"Can we talk privately? This is a bit odd."

"Of course." Laban looked at D'vhan enquiringly. "Can we step into the Red Lodge? The hunters are out and no one will look for me there."

D'vhan gestured at the flap, and they all ducked to enter the Lodge. Siann checked the Lodge for other warriors, ill or resting, and once she was sure the place was empty, undid the pegs holding the hide door and let it drop, sealing them in.

"It's the stone I found on the high plains," Siann explained. Laban looked at the stone and back at Siann quizzically. Siann rubbed the crystal between her hands, watching the blood-red light reflect on the roof of the Lodge.

Laban stretched out his hand hesitantly toward the stone, but the light at its heart died to an ember as soon as he touched it. "It has obviously been keyed to you," he said, "maybe it activated because of the Timiat, but whatever it is, you are the one chosen to wield it. I would like you to bring it to the meeting of Shaman tomorrow, see if any of them has seen such a stone before." Laban looked thoughtful. "We'll tell them about it shining. I don't think we'll discuss the possibility of it vibrating in warning or having any other powers yet. It may be a bit much until we have an explanation."

Siann nodded at Laban, but turned to D'vhan and queried, "Has Y'keta spoken to you about this?"

D'vhan shrugged, scratching idly at the scraggly red beard he had been unsuccessfully attempting to grow all winter. "He told me before first meal something was making him uneasy. I thought it was the presence of so many strangers in camp. Why do you ask?"

"He said he wanted to talk to you before he came with me to speak to Laban about the stone." Siann's eyes narrowed. "I wonder what the annoying hatchling is up to this time."

Laban's eyes twinkled as he reached to open the flap to leave the Lodge. "I never see you two do anything but argue. I think you should marry him."

Siann shivered and stuck a very grown-up tongue out at the shaman. "Don't you even speak such words. We'd kill each other before the ceremony ended!"

They walked out into the pale sunshine, laughing.

§

Y'keta sat immobile, hidden in the shadow of one of the outer tents, waiting for D'vhan, Laban, and Siann to go into the Red Lodge. Shaking his numb legs, he grabbed a travel bag of drymeat and berries. Stamping to get rid of the pins and needles, he headed into the forest.

For an hour, he headed east, keeping to the game trails where any scouting party he met would expect to find a warrior on the hunt. A few hours from the Village, he broke through the thick brush as carefully as possible and started up the north ridge.

Walking to the foot of the mountains would take most of the day, but he was counting on Surta's distrust of anyone approaching their area to save him the journey, and it did.

After a few hours of hard climbing up and down ridges, always heading north, Y'keta heard a rustle behind him and turned to find Oryel, one of the Roost guardians peering down his tawny beak at Y'keta.

"Greetings Oryel, how fares the Roost?" The chill breeze ruffled Oryel's feathers and made Y'keta rub his cold arms. "I need to speak to my father. It's a matter of urgency."

Oryel stared, and took off. *Most likely on his way to report in*, Y'keta thought. Never the most companionable of birds, the silence was odd even for Oryel. Shrugging, he scrambled up the next ridge, still headed towards the Roost.

A black shadow flew overhead and suddenly Surta was there. "Y'keta, Oryel reported to the Council. You needed to speak to me?"

Here it is, Y'keta thought, trying to keep his emotions under control. Swallowing the fireball of anger dealing with his father always seemed to bring, he said, "I come to ask your help, as head of the Roost." He used the formal words of supplication, putting it on the level of Council business rather than a personal level. "The Utlaak will attack Esquialt in three days. The villagers are weak from the hard winter and short on supplies." He bowed his head, wrapping his arms around himself as he forced the words past the pride blocking his craw. "I ask that the Roost do what it can to help them."

Surta nodded approvingly. "You were wise to return before the attack." He turned, took to the air, and spoke to Y'keta over his shoulder as he ascended, "I will send a pair of guards to escort you back to the Roost."

"You don't understand, A'ta," Y'keta said, "I'm not coming back to the Roost. I'm returning to the Village to face the attack."

Surta spun around, landing with a thud not three feet from Y'keta. Peering down his black beak derisively, he probed, "And what will you do? You admitted the Village is weak. You will stay here, where you belong."

"The Utlaak will attack, most likely at the end of the Winter Festival, which begins today," Y'keta said. "I will be there. It is my place."

The cold winds whipped through Y'keta's clothes and left his arms and legs shivering. *This is no place for someone without feathers,* he thought.

Surta's beak snapped together loudly enough to send a shower of loose snow falling from the overhanging branches. "This is your place! Here, with me. You are my son. You will be the chief of our people. What will happen to the Roost if the Utlaak destroy you?"

"No, Ata!" Y'keta stood on the snow-covered bluff, looking down on Esquialt as the Village sat unconcernedly in the valley. "I'm going back."

Lightning crackled in Surta's black eyes as he glared at his wayward hatchling. "Now, Y'keta..."

"No, A'ta, just this once listen to me!" Y'keta's voice broke but he stood his ground, trying to ignore the flashes of lightning bouncing around the hills, visible signs of Surta's anger. "You sent me to the villagers to learn, and one of the things I learned is not to walk away from responsibility just because it scares me."

Y'keta could hear the argument from night he had been banished echoing in his mind.

"I will be here should you need me." Surta had said. And now, when Surta was truly needed, he was turning away, as usual.

§

"I know you are concerned about the attack, Y'keta." Surta spoke calmly, trying to reach past the defiance in Y'keta's yellow glare. "And I know you have developed attachments with some of the villagers."

Y'keta snorted. "Attachments? You make it sound like I had contracted feather-rot, or lice. These *attachments* are my friends. I have lived with them, hunted and fought with them, gone hungry in the winter and thirsty in the summer drought. That is what you sent me there to do, to learn how to belong. I am going." There was no anger in Y'keta's voice, but it echoed with a determination Surta could not break. "I will send word if things go well. If not, I will greet you when we meet on the Sky Road."

Turning from his father, Y'keta began his climb down the mountain. The light faded as the air became thicker and the aspens and larches replaced the pine trees.

§

Soon he switched to a ground-eating trot and let his mind prepare for the day to come. The Winter Ceremony was the climax of the ceremonial year. Shaman would come from all the neighbouring villages, and for three days there would be feasting, ceremonies, and merriment. On the third day, there would be a reading of the Scrolls. He remembered Siann walking across the circle between the lodges, staring at the scroll she was to read and muttering to herself. She had been so focused that she walked right into Pey't without even realising it. She had bounced off his broad belly like a pebble bouncing down a hill, and carried on towards the Grey Lodge, muttering under her breath. Pey't had simply laughed, his soft, fleshy face jiggling.

Footsore and cold in body and heart, Y'keta finally reached the Village. A part of him was still hoping to see one of the guards fly overhead or to see his fatherland and offer his support, but that didn't happen. *I should have known*, he thought, the betrayal biting worse than the wind. He slowly worked his way through the crowd of villagers and over to where Laban and D'vhan were standing near the central campfire. They were talking with Shaman from the other villages, but when they saw the quiet concern on his face, they broke off discussions and steered him away from the group to a spot in the darkness between lodges.

Y'keta stood in front of D'vhan and Laban, straightened his red festival tunic, and tried to calm the herd of buffalo stampeding in his stomach. "They will attack at the end of the festival." He stared at D'vhan, willing the older warrior to believe him. "The Shaman and warriors from the other tribes will leave. We will be alone, and weak from the long winter, our elders and children vulnerable."

Laban poked a stick at the meagre day fire. "Why not now," he said. "What have you seen that the Elders have not?"

"May I?" Y'keta gestured at the scorched stick Laban held. Taking it from his outstretched hand, he used the charcoaled end to draw images in the dry, cracked earth before the fire.

"Look." He drew a broad squiggle in the dust. "This is the river and the coastline near Atiskaat." He quickly sketched a few lodge shapes. "This is here, our principal winter camp, sheltered from the winds by the mountains." His young voice cracked as he willed the two Elders to understand. "The mountains are full of tunnels and Utlaak burrows. We know about this from when I was captured. I am sure they will attack now, the majority of the snow has gone so the entrances to their tunnels are open, but we are still weak. Our warriors range days from camp because we are short of supplies. We are undefended. During the winter, they couldn't attack because of the snow. Remember, they are not weak. I've seen those tunnels, they are stacked with supplies and weapons enough for years of war."

"I know all this, Hatchling." D'vhan's voice still sounded wispy from the lung fever that had burned through the camp over the winter. "But how do you know they will come at the end of

the festival? Not next week, or tonight, or last
moon."

"For the last year, you have lectured me
over and over about accepting the voices I hear
in the wind, told me to learn from the Buffalo
and the Wolf." Y'keta's strange eyes burned
earnestly in the dimness between the lodges.
"Well, I'm listening. The Wolf says they will
attack after the visiting warriors have left. The
Buffalo says to move the calves to safety. It is
coming, old crow, please believe me!"

D'vhan nodded suddenly. "I feel it, child."
He turned to Laban, addressing him formally.
"Salixt, after the ceremony tomorrow, we must
move the Green and Grey Lodges to safety.
Y'keta, gather the Reds and collect firewood
and all the oil you can find. We will have work
to do, but keep it quiet, there is no reason to let
them see we are preparing."

Twenty-Five

Celebration and Preparation
<<<Siann>>>

The next day bustled with noise and celebration. The children of Esquialt ran around the campsite like mad calves, mowing down any slow-moving elders and leaving a swirl of dust and laughter wherever their herd roamed.

The Elders and the Mothers traded with each other for herbs and rare foodstuffs, and the nose-pinching smells of Silvergrass and Camas filled the air around the Green Lodge fires.

Since last spring, when I saw proof that the Waki'tani existed and for some reason were watching over our Village, the world had become a much bigger and much scarier place than I ever thought it could be. My fingers tingled as I reached into my pack and touched the oddly shaped crystal. I carried the stone everywhere now, rubbed it, turned it over and over in my palms. It was becoming an obsession. Whenever I thought no one was looking, I would pull it out and peer into the brilliant red depths. Staring into the fire that wouldn't shine for anyone but me.

Laban had told me to keep it secret, in case someone superstitious saw it and was frightened. But after Y'keta warned us that an Utlaak attack was coming either tonight or tomorrow, I hadn't been able to leave the stone in my lodge. I wasn't going to miss the warning this time. It was nearly time for me to stand before the central campfire and read the Scroll of the Waki'tani. I had practiced for six moons, ever since Mother told me I would be reading it. Back in the spring, when the world was safe, and my mother's wrath was the only thing to fear. But between losing Maskim, the warning stone, and now the rumours of attack, I hadn't been able to concentrate on the ceremony. All these things made reading an outdated scroll for a bunch of Shaman who hadn't seen what I had seen rather unimpressive.

"What are you brooding over, Hatchling?" Y'keta's nasal voice interrupted, as usual. "You look like you've got prickle bushes in your shoes."

"I'm getting ready for tonight's reading." I tried to keep my voice even. I didn't want to give any clue to the annoying warrior that I thought something tied him to the Waki'tani scroll. I still wasn't sure. So many strange things had happened since he came to the Village in the spring, it made me suspicious.

"It's time for the Ceremony," he badgered. "Brood later, celebrate now."

Shaking the scroll at his retreating back, I walked towards the soft drumbeats coming from the centre of the camp.

§

"As always, we finish this festival with a reading of the Scroll of the Waki'tani. We remember the wars of our past and the intervention of the Sky Lords. But this year, there is more, for the enemy of our past has returned. Atiskaat was attacked without provocation. Varas came to us after his village was destroyed. We were attacked coming back from the summer camp." Laban paced around the fire as he reeled off the string of Utlaak attacks and the loss and devastation it had caused. "It would be easy to despair," he said, "to think we had been forgotten. But it is not so. The Sky Lords watch us still." His arm gestured at the Sky Road shining overhead. "Tonight we hear and remember; remember our past, remember our losses, and remember that our future shines like the Dancers of the North, if we Walk into it together."

Laban turned to me and bowed deeply. "Siann is our newest shaman. She walked the

Lightning when her mother left us in the fall. She will read the Scroll of the Waki'tani."

I stood up, nervously pulling my tunic straight, then taking the much-studied scroll from the bag beside me, I began. "As a child, I was not sure if I believed the words of this scroll. I thought the legends were only there to make a bloody part of our history easier for the children and the elders." My eyes drifted over the villagers I'd known all my life and the visiting Shaman, most of whom I had never met. "I have seen the Sky Lords watching this village, I know the words of this scroll are true!" With that startling announcement, I began to recite, "In the depths of our winter, the Utlaak came..." The recitation was long, but I could feel every eye fixed on me as I told the ancient story of the last war with the Utlaak. Finally, I handed the scroll back to Laban and returned to my seat beside Napaay in the circle.

"The festival is finished," Laban pronounced, "and the night is almost done. We have one more task, a more joyful one, before we end this night. Iamaat, please ask Ren Ut'yaat if she would join us."

Iamaat walked over to the Red Lodge. I was surprised to see that the ceremonial hide blocked the door. That door was seldom closed before nightfall. The warriors allowed anyone entrance to their home.

I heard Laban gasp as Ren walked out of the Red Lodge, a long cloak of raven feathers sweeping behind her. Her pale hair shone in the moonlight, the bright-red beads woven through her intricate hairstyle sending echoes of flame dancing around the fire. Drums beat softly from the darkness beyond the campfire.

Ren stepped forward, circling the campfire in time with the heartbeat drums. Step. Step. Stop. With each pause in the rhythm, her eyes sought out Laban standing at the centre of the fire circle. The air was cold and clear, each breath visible in the night. Spreading the black wings of her cloak, she circled around the fire three times and returned to kneel before Laban.

Laban's soft voice filled the fire circle, drifting like smoke between the trees. "Ren Ut'yaat. Lady of the mysterious eyes, who's heart has become my home. May I say in front of these witnesses and with the Elder Stars hearing my vows." Kneeling to meet her, Laban picked up her hands and held them in his warm grasp. "The stars shine in your eyes."

"Our Roads have always been one," Ren responded.

Iamaat, as the eldest Mother of the Village, reached between them and tied them together. The three sacred ribbons—green for life, brown for the earth, blue for the sky—wove an intricate pattern around their joined hands.

"Your paths are one," she said. "The Elder Stars witness it. Each day you wake, you wake together. Each night you sleep, you sleep together. Cry together, love together, and when the call comes, Walk together onto the Sky Road."

D'vhan grabbed Ren by the shoulders and Savohn of Atiskaat grabbed Laban. They pulled hard, trying to separate the new couple, but Iamaat knew her job—the bindings held. They pulled, again and again, three times, once for the earth, once for the sky, and once for the Elder Stars.

"The bindings held," D'vhan smiled broadly. "Their souls are one before the sky."

"The bindings held." Savohn grinned at Laban. "Their souls are one before the earth."

"The bindings held. Their souls are one." Iamaat completed the ritual, "The Elder Stars have witnessed it."

A cry went up from the assembled villagers as Ren and Laban were surrounded by well-wishers. Laban let the clamour die down for a few minutes before rising in front of the fire and calling for quiet. "We are thankful for the joy we share today," he proclaimed, his calm grey eyes drifting over the crowd. "But there has been battle and loss this year, as there has not been for cycles uncounted." Silence fell around the campsite, forming itself to the depths of

Laban's calm voice. His brow wrinkled and, for the first time, he seemed to hesitate as he addressed the quiet crowd. "We believe there may be an attack tomorrow at nightfall." Cries of fear and defiance roared around the campfire, making Laban raise his voice to continue. "We know this may happen and we have prepared. Tomorrow the Green and Grey lodges will leave for Atiskaat. I will not take chances with either our future or our history. Savohn will travel with you. Shaman from the other villages will depart with their warriors."

Laban nodded at Savohn and the other Shaman around the circle. "For tonight, go to your lodges, prepare for leaving, and sleep in the knowledge we have defeated the Utlaak before. This is merely one more battle."

It took a long time for silence to descend on the camp and it was an eerie silence when it did. But eventually, we all slept.

Twenty-Six

Blood Under the Stars

The morning air was full of wailing as the young mothers and the elders protested against Laban's edict. "No," he said. "Our young ones are the future, and the Grey Lodge are our history. We will not risk you."

One by one the great war canoes left for Atiskaat loaded with those with too many winters, or far too few. One of the Mothers guarded each of the canoes.

Thunderheads swirled around the frowning face of Varas as he stood stubbornly beside the final canoe. "Don't do this to me, Laban," he said. "I was too young to fight when the Utlaak destroyed my village, don't make me walk away again!"

Laban rested a firm hand on Varas' shoulder, "You are of Esquialt now, Varas, and you are of the Green Lodge. The stories of our Village and all the stories of your home village

are in your care. If we lose you, both histories
may die. Be done. Go."

A heavy silence descended on the Village as
the canoes moved out of the bay and into the
wider ocean.

§

Weapons bristled like pinecones as the warriors
prepared for what could be their first real battle
against the Utlaak.

D'vhan stood near the fire, surrounded by
large piles of firewood and all the cooking oil
from the lodges. "Dig," he said. "We need
trenches around the main Lodges before the
dark falls." Hoes were pulled out of the lodges
and soon all that could be heard was the
chipping of rock and grunts of the warriors as
they hacked at the still-frozen earth, creating a
wheel that ran around the central campfire with
spokes out to the trenches at each main Lodge.

Y'keta looked up at the purpling sky and
wondered if his father would even care about
the battle today. *Would he come?*

The central campfire roared to life as dusk
fell, blazing defiance into the night sky.
"Warriors! Backs to the fire!" D'vhan said.
"Laban, Siann, and all those not of the Red
Feather, stack the firewood in the trenches and
then get into the centre, as near the fire as you
can. Prepare to bandage and heal should any fall

during the battle and, by the Sun of Riad, keep this fire going!"

D'vhan walked around the circle of warriors touching each on the shoulder or speaking a soft word.

"Keep your eyes into the darkness, if you need something from behind, call for it. Do not look back. Your eyes will take too long to adjust." Then, still wheezing, he took his place in front of Laban at the entrance to the Village.

"We are the Guardians. Strength of the sky," D'vhan chanted. Red Lodge joined him, their voices filling the clearing with resolve and defiance.

"We are the Guardians, strength of the sky.

We walk the dark places, fight fear in the night.

Will you walk beside us to serve and to die;
To hold safe the People, keep honour alight
As we take up our spears on the Sky Road."

§

They came with the first star's light. Wave after wave of dark, scaly creatures wielding beautiful, ugly instruments of death. Clubs embedded with razor-sharp crystal shards glinted in the firelight.

The sounds of the battle were horrendous, but it was the smell Y'keta would never forget.

No one warned him about the smell of blood, iron, and burning. His nose wrinkled in disgust and it took everything in him to keep his gorge down. Once again he cursed the sensitivity of human senses. This would never have happened to him before.

He dodged and struck with his dagger again and again. Losing his footing on the blood-soaked ground, he fell at the feet of a large Utlaak carrying a two-handed sword.

Y'keta rolled, coming up right below him and slicing across the Utlaak's exposed stomach. With a sickening pop, the Utlaak collapsed.

Entrails poured over Y'keta. He bolted away, gagging.

A harsh voice bellowed from behind him. "'Keta, down!" Falling flat into the dirt, Y'keta felt a whisper of wind as a crystal-studded club whistled overhead.

"Watch yourself, Hatchling!" D'vhan gave him a swift shove towards the fire-lit circle. "Dead warriors don't save anyone."

"This can't go on," Y'keta said, "they are just too many!"

"Light it!" D'vhan hollered.

Siann smashed the gourd of cooking oil and poured it onto the wood stacked in the trenches. Laban grabbed a burning branch from the campfire, igniting the oil-drenched wood in each spoke.

Utlaak tripped over each other as they blinked wildly in the sudden blaze.

Lighting arrows from the central fire, Ren yelled, "Throw!" Pey't hurled small jars at the blinded enemy.

Ren's arrows didn't miss. Fire arrows smashed and then ignited the liquid in the small gourds. The night filled with the howling of the injured and the stench of burning flesh.

Utlaak dropped to the ground, desperately trying to smother the mixture of honey and burning oil that splattered from each jar.

There was plenty of courage, D'vhan thought, *just not enough time.*

Even injured the Utlaak kept coming. Whatever pushed them from behind was worse than the burning oil and the brightness of the clearing.

The warriors would not last until dawn.

Screaming erupted from the rear of the attacking horde—tripping over each other in desperation—the Utlaak ran into the clearing, heedless of the fire and the arrows.

The villagers were forgotten as large black shapes appeared on the outskirts of the fight.

Y'keta saw them first—Surta and the guards of the Roost. Sword strokes flashing cold in the starlight. They had come.

The Utlaak were trapped between the arrows of the Village and the swords of the Waki'tani.

Metal tipped talons flashed in the moonlight. Tall silhouettes circled outside the firelight — forcing the Utlaak closer and closer to the arrows of the Villagers.

It was brief, brutal, bloody, and it was over.

The villagers stared at Surta and the guards as they stood at the edge of the firelight, cleaning swords and tending to the minor wounds they had taken.

Siann stepped over the corpses of the dead and away from the campfire, stopping halfway to the group of Waki'tani. "I know you," she addressed the large black figure of Surta. The avian head turned towards her, beak snapping. "I saw you in the spring, on the ridge above our camp. You were watching us."

He shrugged dismissively, feathers whispering in the cool night, and turned back to his own people.

Either braver than the rest or more desperate, one of the injured Utlaak jumped up close to where Siann stood staring disconsolately at Surta's retreating form. With a howl of grief and defiance, it heaved the crystal-shard mace at her undefended back.

Y'keta flew between the mace and Siann. The crystal-studded weapon struck him in the chest, blood and feathers flying as it hit.

An anguished scream pierced the night. Blades flashed and the Utlaak collapsed, this time permanently.

Silence fell. Blood and feathers fell. Blood. And. Feathers.

Twenty-Seven

Revelations and Consequences

Siann bent over the bloody mass that was once Y'keta's ribcage, now caved in by the Utlaak mace. The blow he had taken for her. He was dying for her.

He didn't love her. Shards, they didn't even like each other most of the time! But he was dying…for her.

No one moved. Time itself froze into a chilling tableau where the red stain on Y'keta's tunic grew a beat at a time as his shattered heart pumped wildly, trying to keep life flowing in a body so utterly broken.

Pulling her cape from her shoulders, Siann dropped to her knees and gently settled it over Y'keta's chest, hiding the bloody green feathers that meant the end of his life in the Village.

A shadow, darker than the darkness, loomed over her, and she looked up into the eyes of the black Raven Lord. "He died for me," she choked out. "He didn't need to. I knew too much, it was safer for him to let me die, but he saved me."

The tip of a black wing traced Y'keta's ashen face. "My son," he whispered, the whistles and clicks making his voice clipped and emotionless. "Fly to the Elder Stars, Y'keta. Greet your mother and sister well for me."

A tingling in the centre of her chest distracted Siann from her grief. She reached to pull out the thong holding the fiery crystal.

"What is this?" Surta said, "No Walker has ever held a—" the word was indecipherable, a series of low clicks and chirps. "Where did you get the crystal?"

"This came to me when my mother died," Siann said. "It has warned us of attacks. It is how the Village knew that the Utlaak would come tonight."

"Can you use the Stone, Groundling?" Surta's voice was urgent, words almost indecipherable amid the high-pitched whistles. "Does it burn for you?"

D'vhan and Laban walked up and joined them. Slow tears washed away the caked-on mud and blood on D'vhan's face as he looked at Y'keta's grey form cooling in the dirt. Siann was so far out of her depths, she looked to Laban, who nodded slightly. "Yes," she said, "it burns for me."

"Use the light." Surta whistled in agitation. "Quickly, before it is too late. Call the fire and heal my son!" Laban and D'vhan looked from Y'keta to Surta with shocked comprehension. Siann wasn't sure. She had never heard of this use for any sacred stone. Everything it had done so far had been passive—it warned about attacks, it didn't prevent them. Rubbing the crystal between her hands, she waited for the familiar tingle telling her the stone was waking. Embracing the current that flowed through her, she thought about Y'keta. About him diving in front of the Utlaak's mace, about him searching for D'vhan in the frozen winter, all the things about him that didn't irritate her. She wished him well and whole.

The stone between her hands took fire. A bright red beam shot between her clenched fingers and settled around Y'keta, enveloping his body in a flickering inferno. He convulsed, his body shaking so hard that Siann thought she heard bones break. The light darkened to the colour of old blood. Focusing on his chest, she saw it move though his flailed ribs, rebuilding tissue and reforming bone. His heart beat once, stuttered, and took up its regular rhythm. Fire faded from the stone and Siann collapsed across Y'keta's unconscious form.

Surta looked at the shaman and the warrior. Both of whom had heard Y'keta's secret. "He will heal," Surta said. "She will be well." He withdrew a few paces, turning back to say, "There is power in her she has not tapped yet. Guard her well, the Utlaak will come for her." The black wings stretched against the dark sky and he was gone. No answers given.

Twenty-Eight

The Path that is Before Me

Siann pried her gritty eyelids open. Her mouth tasted like something furry had crawled in there to die. Slowly she turned her head from left to right, but even those small movements felt like they had earned her a nap. Breathing in the sweetgrass and peppermint smell of the healer's hut, she slept.

§

Y'keta woke to the knowledge of pain. He guessed his chest was healing. It must be, or he would be dead by now. *What was I thinking,* he chided himself. *Shards, I've blown it this time! Siann saw everything.* Of course it had to be her. The shell-headed hatchling was much too quick to have missed seeing his feathers. She would be busy putting clues together and getting him kicked out of the Village. Still, no matter what happened now, the Village was saved and the burrow had hurt much worse. Slowly, he lifted his aching head, peering around the

Healers' Lodge. The air was heavy with the essence of peppermint and the other herbs the healers poured into kettles of hot water, creating steam that left an oily taste in his mouth.

"Are you awake, Hatchling?" D'vhan's voice came from the pallet next to him. The warrior leader was stretched out under a thin hide blanket and leant up on one elbow to watch Y'keta through the potent smoky haze.

Y'keta froze. The low tone seemed filled with concern, not at all how he expected D'vhan to respond. What if Siann hadn't told them? Images taunted him of the person he'd been when he arrived last spring. He remembered challenging Surta and Matra, feeling like an outcast from his own people, and oh so superior to the Mud Walkers. Had he ever called them that? Slow, salty tears dribbled from his eyes. For the first time in his life, he felt like these people believed in him. They had valued him not as the chief's son but for himself. Now his heart was breaking at the thought of losing them.

"Hear me, Y'keta." D'vhan's voice was insistent, but quiet enough not to wake any of the other wounded who were sleeping in the lodge. "You are Red Lodge, a warrior under my command. Nothing changes." He paused and then muttered again, as though to convince himself, "Nothing changes."

"How could it not change?" Y'keta whispered, "I lied to you, about everything."

"You didn't." D'vhan's amused voice sounded close in the darkness. "You were cast out by your chief, is that a lie?"

"No, but—"

"You pledged yourself to become Kit'na to the Village, was that a lie?"

"No, but—"

"So stop squawking. You did not lie." D'vhan's voice had taken on the teacher tone Y'keta had come to know and dislike. "What is the essence of becoming Kit'na?"

"Stop it, old crow!" Y'keta snapped, this wasn't the time for games and logic problems. He was in pain and his world was collapsing.

Black eyes flashed angrily. "Listen to me!" D'vhan said, his eyes snapping with dark fire. "You know I am from Atiskaat. I left the village and all I knew there to become Kit'na and join my Road with Esquialt. Pey't was from one of the mountain villages in the north lands. We all come from somewhere."

"But not somewhere like I do," Y'keta almost spat the words at D'vhan, his querulous voice shaking. He had built this confrontation up in his head for the last full cycle. Rehearsed it every time he had set a foot wrong or thought Siann was getting too close to the truth. For D'vhan to say it didn't matter was insulting. He squinted, covering his eyes reflexively as a shaft of sunlight invaded the room. Two indistinct forms entered the lodge and quickly closed the flap behind them, sealing in the fragrant smoke and steam. Squatting in front of Y'keta's pallet, one of the visitors turned out to be Laban. The other was a tall, gaunt man Y'keta didn't recognise, perhaps one of the Shaman from the other villages.

The tall man leant over, putting a long-fingered hand against Y'keta's flushed cheeks. "You are still feverish, my son, but at least you are awake."

"A'ta?" Y'keta could never forget that voice. It was the first one he had ever learned. "How can you be here?"

Surta looked at Laban, who quickly checked that no one was in hearing distance, and nodded. "Your friends agreed to let me come into the Village to make sure you were mending. You seem to be doing well."

"I'm not sure why," Y'keta marvelled. "As soon as the mace hit me I knew I was dying." Weakly raising one arm, Y'keta touched the centre of his chest where broken bones and shattered flesh had been. It hurt, shards it hurt, but he could breathe and there didn't seem to be any more blood.

"It was Siann," Laban told him. "She healed you using the fiery stone."

"I have never seen one of the Walkers—" Surta looked slightly embarrassed, "my apologies, Laban, I know no other name for your people. I have never seen a power stone used by your people before. She paid a high price for your life, my son."

"Will she recover, A'ta?" It felt so strange to be speaking to his father in front of the Elders. His world had slipped out of phase and he didn't understand the rules anymore.

"It will take time, my son. If the Stone works for her people the way it has for ours, she will need several weeks to rebuild her strength. Sparing your life drained hers."

Surta turned to Laban and nodded politely. "We call the Stone—" he looked at Y'keta and gave out a series of high-pitched whistles and clicks.

"Life Binder," Y'keta translated.

"My thanks." Surta nodded at Y'keta. "The Life Binder Stone physically binds the life essence of one being to another's aid, draining the girl's life to replenish Y'keta's. It will always be dangerous, Laban, and should be used to heal only in the direst need."

Laban glanced back towards the family area of the Healers' Lodge, where Siann had slept almost constantly for the past few days. "She wakes for a few moments each day, but tires easily."

"I need to talk to her, to make sure she will be all right," Y'keta demanded, remembering the Spring Festival last year and Siann standing up to the Elders to earn him a place in the Village. He owed her. Much as the hatchling annoyed him on a daily basis, he owed her.

Surta peered at Laban and D'vhan. "May I speak with my son privately?" They nodded and stepped out of the lodge, leaving Surta and Y'keta alone. Thunderheads started forming in Y'keta's stomach, churning and churning until he could taste the acid climbing into his gullet.

Surta started, "Y'keta, you were right, your friends are people of honour who were deserving of our protection."

This was hardly the way Y'keta thought this conversation was going to go. "They have been good friends to me, A'ta. I have learned a great deal about the People this year."

"Your decision to risk yourself to save the shaman girl was admirable, Y'keta, but could have proven foolish."

Now it comes, Y'keta thought, waiting for the sparks to light in his father's eyes.

"It didn't, though, and a valuable person was saved because of your actions." Suddenly Surta drew himself to his full height and Y'keta took a steadying breath to prepare for the battle he knew was coming. "But now it's time for you to come home. The Council has lifted your banishment and you can return to the Roost." It wasn't a question, it wasn't even an order, it was pure assumption. Surta turned to walk out of the lodge, not even looking to see if Y'keta was behind him. Y'keta would obey because, in Surta's mind, there was no other choice.

"Thank the Council well for me, my father, but I will not be returning to the Roost now. Maybe not ever." It took every piece of courage Y'keta could find not to let his voice quaver as he spoke. "You sent me to the Village to learn how to belong. I belong here now. I will not abandon them."

The black leathers Surta wore in his humanoid form seemed to ripple in an unfelt wind, and lightning was flashing in his eyes. "You are my son and heir, you are a Waki'tani and under my command. You will go where I send you!"

"No, my father." Y'keta marshalled all the arguments he had prepared for this day, hoping some part of his father could hear him. "You sent me here to learn. Will you listen to the things I have learned, will you hear who I am, before you tell me who I should be?"

"You are my son. I think I know who you are." Surta's voice held echoes of closed doors and locked rooms, immovable.

"I am not the hatchling that you sent away last spring," Y'keta insisted. "I am Red Lodge,

Buffalo's Child, Waki'tani, Prisoner of the Utlaak…each of these things has changed me, given me a voice that you must hear."

"I will hear you when you stand in our Roost in your own form. Then we will see how much of this Village remains in you."

"I came as Kit'na to this village. To become Kit'na, I left my home and dedicated myself to walking the Road with these people until the Sky Lords release me to join the Elder Stars. This decision you forced upon me because you would not see who I am, only who you needed me to be." He took a deep breath and continued before Surta could interrupt, "I am not Netta. Her death was tragic, and partly my fault, but even before she was taken, I was not like her. She was born to be the heir of the Roost, I was not. There are other Councillors you trust more than I, who know more, and care more, about the Waki'tani than I am capable of. One of them can follow you, or one of Netta's hatchlings when they are older. You are already training them. I know you are. She lived for the Roost and died for the Roost as I now live for this village and, if necessary, will give my life up for it."

Surta didn't speak right away. He rose up to his full height, seeming to dominate the large main room of the lodge. Bowing his dark head, he looked at Y'keta as though he were a stranger. "This decision of yours is not without consequence. If you deny the Roost, the Roost will deny you. There will be no more help from the Waki'tani."

"I deny no one, my father. I'm proud of my heritage as Waki'tani," Y'keta said. He was desperate to ease the pain he saw in his father's cold eyes, but he knew if he wavered now all he had gained in the last year would be lost. "You will never know how proud I am to be your son, but I will never be Chief of the Waki'tani. It is not my nature. I walk the path the Stars have laid before me. I can do no other."

Surta seemed to shrink inward on himself, and for the first time Y'keta saw the years his father had carried the burden of the Roost. The price he paid for his people. "You know where we are should you decide to return. We will not approach the People while you dwell with them. We are not your enemies, but you can no longer consider the Waki'tani as allies of the People." The ultimatum, given in a flat, dead voice was full of unspoken pain. Turning abruptly, Surta walked out of the lodge and, without paying attention to who may see his transformation, dropped his human illusion and soared into the darkness.

Y'keta watched as the black speck that had been his father faded into the distance. He mourned, maybe he would always mourn, for the sorrow his choice had caused, but the People of the Village were his responsibility and he would never abandon them.

War was coming.

Guardian

Coming Soon

Decisions can come back to haunt you.

Five cycles ago Y'keta's fear of the responsibility of being the chief's son drove him into exile. Now, in a different place he must face that choice again.

The Utlaak horde is on the move, burning village after village as they search for the mysterious Lifebinder crystal and Siann, the young shaman who controls it.

One day soon they will find his village, and her. On that day Y'keta must decide if he can accept losing everything he has come to love or if he will finally become what he was meant to be. The Guardian.

To my readers

Thank you for sharing Y'keta's Road with me.

I'd love to hear from you, so please check me out on social media.

Facebook - @SandraHurst.Author
Twitter -   @_SandraHurst
Website: www.delusionsofliteracy.com

If you enjoyed this book, please let others know. Most people will trust the word of a friend over any amount of advertising.

Also, leave a review! I love to hear your opinions, which parts you enjoyed most, and what you think of the Sky Road.

Thank you for walking the Sky Road with me. I look forward to seeing you for the next adventure.

... Sandra

Acknowledgements

Y'keta owes itself to so many people.

Ever and always to Mike and Cameron, who put up with me during the labour pains, ate cold pizza more times that I'll admit, and learned that "I'll be coming to bed soon," is writer's shorthand for, "see you in the morning."

To Maida who made me think about identity and the costs of being real.

To Taija, who edited my baboon droppings into real sentences, and Rebecca who convinced me that maybe they weren't baboon droppings to begin with. And to the amazing, supportive writers' community in Calgary who taught me, encouraged me, and wouldn't let me quit.

Cover art by: AprilVolition Design

Editing by: T.J. Morgan Editing

About the Author

As a child growing up in England, stories and legends surrounded me. When I was 8, we moved to northern Canada and the legends changed. Stories of the Fae and the little people, were replaced by legends of the Thunderbird and stories of the woodlands. I never stood a chance. What could I be but a writer?

Growing up in Northern Alberta gave me a great love and respect for the wild lands and indigenous cultures which made its way into the worlds I create. A mythmaker at heart, I started writing poetry in middle school and graduated to epic fantasy.

My first book, *Y'keta*, is loosely based on the Thunderbird of North American legend, Y'keta is a Young Adult, high fantasy set in an ancient world where legends walk and the Sky Road offers a way to the stars.

I now live in Calgary, Alberta with my husband and son, both of whom I love dearly and have put up for sale on e-bay when their behaviour demanded it.

How do I say that?

The language of the People borrows liberally from several modern native languages which I have 'aged' in different directions to suit the Sky Road. Pronunciation can therefore be as varied and quirky as the People themselves.

The Walkers

In Esquialt (Eskwee-alt)

Siann (*See*-ahn)	Daughter of the Shaman
Matra (Matra)	Head Shaman, Grey Lodge
D'vhan (*D*-vaan)	Warrior Leader, Red Lodge
Iamaat (**E***a*-mat)	Green Lodge Leader
Y'keta (yuh-**Kee***t*a) arrived	A new warrior, recently
Pey't (Payt)	Warrior, Red Lodge
Saweia (Sah-weeah)	Warrior, Red Lodge
Hahnee (Hah-nee)	Shaman-Grey Lodge
Savohn (Suv-ohn)	Shaman- Grey Lodge

In Atiskaat (Atis-Caht)

Siamaat(See-a-mat) Lodge	Shaman - Atiskaat, Grey
Amakil (am-a-kill)	Hunter from Atiskaat

The Sky Lords

Surta   (*Sir*-tah)   Chief of the Sky Lords
Oryel (or-**yell**)   Roost Guardian

Other Vocabulary

Kit'na (**Kit**-nuh)   Literally, traveller – a
young

                     man/woman who leaves
their

                     own village to join another

Salixt (*say*-lix)   Head shaman of the People,
                     Leader of Grey Lodge

Kalixt (*kay*-lix)   Warrior leader of the
village

                     Leader of Red Lodge

Waki'tani
(Wah-**ki**-tah-nee)   The Sky Lords – avian species
                     The ones who fly between the
                     Walkers' world and the Elder
                     Stars.

Utlaak (**uht**-lak)   Vicious tunnel dwellers. They
                     have attacked the villages
many

                     times through their history.

Hania (han-ear)   Carrion birds

Kuniak (koo-nee-ak) Small dog-like pack hunters

Kaal   (kahl)   deer-like creatures used for
                      Food and hides.

Professional Credits

No author creates in a vacuum, there are always a great many talented people who stand behind the scenes and make the wheels go round.

I wouldn't be here without these people. They are consummate professionals, team players, and above all great friends.

Managed by *Ink-N-Flow Management Group*
www.InkNFlowManagementGroup.com
email:Hello@InkNFlowManagementGroup.com

Cover Design: *Amy Queau – Qdesign*
http://www.qcoverdesign.com/
email:

Editing: T. Morgan Editing Services
http://tmorganediting.weebly.com
email:tmorganediting@gmail.com